THE MEXIA MUSIC MURDERS

A Hal Blaine / Judee Sill Mystery

BY

STEVEN WILCOX

For Allan

ACKNOWLEDGEMENTS

This book could not be possible without the love and support of my wife who has put up with my antics for more than a half-century. I thank those who have read my previous books and still encourage me to commit pen to paper. Alan and I share a love of all things musical, and he provided me with the idea for the book.

Thanks to the fine folks at The Pipeline Workshop and BookCamp for providing much-needed guidance in tightening up my storyline. Thanks to Debbie Holley for trudging through and editing the story, to Becky Seale for cleaning up my spelling. I want to give a special shout-out to my fan club, the faculty, staff, and students at Robinson High School for their support and encouragement. The book would not have been finished without the help of Philip Powell who helped crash through a writer's block. A special thanks to my editor, Kirsty Ridge for her invaluable suggestions and comments.

Each character mentioned is the name of someone connected with the music industry. Music has always been a big part of my life, and this is my way of paying homage.

Finally, dear reader, I thank you for letting go of your hard-earned money and purchasing this book. After all, if it were not for you, we writers would have no purpose in life!

PROLOGUE

MURDER MAY BE defined as the unlawful and premeditated killing of one human being by another. Murder is such an unsightly word. Society has become more creative, choosing to assassinate, or eliminate as alternatives. Most murders warrant very little publicity unless the victim is a person of prominence, the murderer is a person of consequence, or the act is so outlandish and gruesome that it attracts notoriety on its own. Sometimes the killing does not become important for years, even decades, when it is discovered to be part of a pattern. That quiet little murder failing to earn more than a few lines in the paper suddenly becomes larger than life when it is part of a pattern. When the murderer is determined to be a serial killer.

Such is the murder of an old man in Paris, 1982. It happened in March with a chilly wind blowing, making the river choppy. Anyone passing this spot would hear the ripples hitting the riverbank. The air was damp and filled with the acrid aroma of dead fish.

The old man had a cane and had his dog on a leash. He suffered from palsy and the cane shook as he walked. His left foot tended to drag. He wore hard-soled shoes, giving his walk a distinct sound. His right foot made a noisy contact as it hit the cobble-stoned pavement, followed by a soft, sliding sound. He walked his dog along this portion of the Rue de la Mer every night. The two found the emptiness of the street comforting.

The old man lived in a house facing an alley behind the

shops, making up a commercial district. Although the dog meandered with curiosity along the path, stopping to sniff a particular stone or a piece of trash, it seldom made a noise. The man would talk with his four-legged companion. Occasionally, he would encourage the dog along by calling, "My Petit Lion."

Otherwise, the pair strolled in silence. Without warning, the old man would stop, speak to his dog and puff on the cigar held in his right hand. He enjoyed looking out over the river. His beret did not cover his balding head and stray gray hair was visible, though his clothes were always neat and clean. He owned two or three threadbare ensembles. Anyone observing the two would assume the old man got lost in some deep, philosophical thought.

Few pedestrians risked walking the Rue de la Mer at night. The street was not well lit, fostering its violent reputation. Although the duo did not encounter another pedestrian, they were not alone. Another man walked behind the old man wearing a dark coat. This second man appeared more of a shadow than a person. He was younger, thinner, and with a full head of dark hair. The shadow walked with determination, faster than the old man. When the shadow was five paces behind, he reached into his right coat pocket and pulled out a pistol. There was a cylinder attached to the gun.

The shadow looked round and confirmed they were alone. Reaching out, he tapped the old man. Startled, the old man turned around, caught sight of the gun, and raised his hand holding the cane. Was this a gesture of surrender? A futile attempt to stop the bullet? Or was it an attempt to deflect the pistol? We will never know.

The shadow shot the old man just above the heart. His victim fell to his knees, failing to process what was happening. Then the shadow pushed the old man backwards, causing him to fall on the dog's leash, preventing the dog from running.

The shadow leaned over and smiled. His target was bleeding out with mouth agape and eyes wide in disbelief. The attacker placed his pistol an inch above the man's face. A myriad of emotions raced through the old man's mind. His lips were moving but nothing came forth.

With a soft whistle, the bullet traveled through the cylinder and entered the old man's forehead, lodging itself in his brain. The shadow then took a piece of paper out of his breast shirt pocket and stuffed it in the dead man's mouth.

* * *

Claude Boiling operated a small machine repair shop along the Rue de la Mer. He arrived at 6:15 a.m. and noticed a dog sitting on the pavement. It wasn't moving and beside it was a heap of clothes. He ambled toward the clothing on the street and approached the dog. The dog never moved. That's when Claude saw it. A man with a hole between his eyebrows. Something was stuffed in the dead man's mouth.

Claude ran back to his store and called the police. By the time the police arrived, other store owners and workers had arrived. They gathered in small crowds, talking among themselves.

"I can't believe this. After all, this is 1982, not 1932!" And with that, they shared stories of organized crime families using the Rue de la Mer to settle disputes in similar ways. The shot was always to the head. Sometimes, they stuffed a warning into the victim's mouth. Sometimes they dropped the body into the river.

Pierre Barouh, the lead detective, had the scene protected as other officers kept bystanders at bay. He and two other detectives had interviewed the bystanders.

"So, you found the body," he began his interview with Claude.

"Not at first. I just noticed the dog." Then looking at the hound asked, "Is he alright? I have some dog food in the store. I forgot to take it home last night for my spaniel."

"The dog does not appear to be injured," he assured the

shopkeeper. "We're taking him to the station, and the animal safety unit will care for him."

"Well, at least that's one thing."

"When did you realize the dog was guarding a body?"

"When I went up to this dog, I expected it to growl or make some noise. But it just sat there in silence. It did not move or make a sound when I approached. That's when I saw the face."

"And what did you do?"

"I ran back to my shop and called you." Claude's voice was full of nervous excitement.

"And did you notice anything in particular about the face?"

"You mean besides something stuffed in the mouth?"

"That is what I meant. Did you recognize what was in his mouth?"

"No, and I didn't stay any longer than I had to. There are rats around here. I thought it might be a rat eating breakfast." The shopkeeper looked around and said, "Rats!"

Claude stood and watched the two white coats from the ambulance load the body.

"Monsieur Bolling, do you know the victim?"

"No. I mean, I have seen him around here. But I can't say I know him. My guess? He lives in one of those houses," pointing to the alleyway behind the shops.

Pierre made notes, closed his notebook, and put it in an inside coat pocket. "Merci," he said and turned to leave.

"Wait," said Claude. "If it wasn't a rat, what was in his mouth?"

"A piece of paper. A note," Pierre replied.

Claude repeated, "A note? What did it say?"

Pierre got out his notebook and looked at his notes, but this was unnecessary. The experience carved the words into his brain.

"C'est pour ma mère."

"C'est pour prendre ma jeunesse."

(This is for my mother. This is for taking my youth.)

Pierre read the note again to himself, ignoring Claude's inquisitive gestures clamoring to know its contents.

"C'est pour ma mère."

"C'est pour prendre ma jeunesse."

Pierre could not ignore the message. The murder was not random, but intentional and personal.

The note did not spell it out, but Pierre had a feeling he knew. Someone had taken a mother from a child or a child from their mother. To no one Pierre asked, "What happened to this mother and this child? Was he kidnapped? Or was she? Or even, and he hesitated, "murdered?" Whose youth did they take?" He looked around him, still thinking out loud. "What happened to this child? Can we find him?"

There were too many unanswerable questions. With others doing their job around him, Pierre stood in front of an abandoned warehouse and again looked at the letter.

C'est pour ma mère

C'est pour prendre ma jeunesse

It jolted him back to reality when the ambulance driver asked, "OK if we leave? Pierre countered, "Where will you take him?"

"Hôtel-Dieu." Pierre was familiar with the Paris morgue.

Without looking at the paper, Pierre handed the note to another officer. The detective walked over to the ambulance and looked inside. He gave a nod, and the driver closed the rear door, walked to the front, climbed inside, and drove off.

* * *

Three weeks later, Pierre brought his chief up to date. His chief was sitting behind his desk.

"I'm sorry, sir. We've hit a brick wall. We learned the old man lived in a boarding house behind the shop. The name he gave the landlord was Auguste Chevalier. A search of all records suggests it may be a fake. I have sent his prints to England and

Interpol, but there is little hope of finding his identity."

"How old was this man?"

Without consulting his notes, Pierre said, "Most likely in his eighties."

"Many people were born at home in his day. There was no law requiring parents to record a birth. Chevalier may or may not be his true name," said the chief. Looking over his steepled fingers at his detective, the chief added, "I doubt you will identify him through public records."

"Right," said Pierre.

"And the note?" the chief asked.

"It suggests a child and their mother were separated cruelly, perhaps via kidnap and enslavement of the child, or maybe someone killed the child's mother, and the child was placed in protective custody. We know how that is."

"Could the shooter be the child in question?" the chief asked.

"Could be," Pierre said in agreement.

"But you don't think so?"

"The murder was professional. Whoever did this is a pro. So, either the child grew up to become a professional assassin, or he ordered someone else to carry it out."

"OK. So, a contract killing?" asked the chief.

"That's my guess, but it still doesn't answer the big questions."

"Who is the mother? Who had their youth stolen?"

"Those are the questions," said Pierre.

"Well, keep me posted." The chief dismissed his detective and resumed reading his morning reports.

Pierre was at his desk boxing up the evidence. Speaking to himself, he said, "Just what I need. Another cold case."

CHAPTER 1

A.C. WAS AN army brat. His family traveled the world as his dad made a career in the army. While stationed at Fort Hood, Texas, his parents met and fell in love. They were married before moving on to the next assignment. While stationed at Fort Bragg, North Carolina, young Anthony C. Mottola entered this world. Upon his father's retirement, the family returned to and settled in North Carolina. Because he moved so many times, A.C. found it easy making friends. After high school, he and a friend moved to Los Angeles where they hoped to be discovered.

While not making it in show business, he found he had a knack for business. A.C. opened a small record store in West Covina, twenty-six miles east of Los Angeles. A.C. kept pace as times and formats changed. He made friends with musicians, record executives and local DJs on KFWB in Hollywood and KRLA in Pasadena. Over the years, A.C. acquired a catalog of rare photos, autographs, and recordings. When the world moved into the digital age, A.C. discovered he had a treasure trove. He had a lot of one-of-a-kind stuff. A.C. believed his collection would become more valuable with time.

* * *

He opened a small recording studio in the back of his store. New acts were welcome to record demos and make it big in the music scene. He also produced commercial jingles for various products and companies. He was the first dealer in Los Angeles with a presence on the internet. His sales exceeded expectations.

In 2010, A.C.'s grandmother asked him to return to Texas.

"Mr. Mottola?" the caller inquired. "This is Anthony Mottola. May I ask who is calling?"

"Mr. Mottola, my name is Mitch Miller, an attorney in Mexia (me HAY e), Texas. Your grandmother, Margaret Ross, is my client. For several months, she has been in declining health. She has requested I reach out to you."

A.C. asked, "Is she alright?"

Mr. Miller said, "That's why I am calling. She isn't doing well and you should come as soon as possible."

"Define as soon as possible."

Miller suggested time was of the essence. "Let me rephrase. How long before you can be here?"

"O.K. I understand. Today is Sunday. I need to clear my calendar and book a flight. I will be there on Monday night. Tuesday morning at the latest."

"Good. I pray there is time for you to say your goodbyes."

There was a pause. A.C. asked, "She is that sick?"

"I am afraid so."

They exchanged more information then A.C. hung up. He took time packing and making a list of things that needed doing before leaving. Then he purchased an open-ended ticket on Southwest from LAX to Dallas' Love Field, rented a car, and made a hotel reservation. The next morning, he closed the store, letting a few friends know about his trip. A.C. was at LAX the required two hours prior to departure.

It was eight that evening when A.C. settled in his hotel room. He got out his cell phone and called the attorney.

"Hello?" the now familiar phone voice said.

"Mr. Miller? This is A.C., Anthony Mottola. You asked me to call when I got in. Where is my grandmother and how is she doing? When can I see her?"

"Remember, Mr. Mottola, "I said your grandmother's condition was grave."

"I remember," said A.C.

The attorney apologized after a pause. "Your grandmother passed away this morning. I tried calling you, but you were unavailable."

There was a long pause. "What now?"

"There isn't much you can do. Your grandmother purchased a pre-arranged funeral. She didn't want to burden you with it. I will take you to the funeral home in the morning. You can visit with the funeral director. He will allow you to have some private time with your grandmother. When did you last see her?"

"I'm not sure. At least three or four years. We sort of drifted apart after Mom died. She wasn't good with cell phones and I wasn't much of a letter writer." There was a pause. "I wish she would have reached out to me sooner. But then, I guess I could have done better with keeping in touch."

Miller waited for A.C. to continue. "I know little about family relationships. I know she was very proud of you."

"Thank you," said A.C.

"You are her only grandchild, and her sole heir. In the morning, I will pick you up. We can go to the funeral home. Where are you staying?

"Holiday Inn."

"Great. I will pick you up. Everything else can wait until after that."

* * *

After A.C. said his goodbyes to his grandmother and spoke with the funeral director, he met Miller at his office. Miller explained, "Mr. Mottola, Mexia is a small town with a population of about 6,800. Although it is the largest city in the county, the county seat is 12 miles to the south along highway 14 in Groesbeck. It is about half the size of Mexia. Our downtown follows U.S. 84, a major east-west artery stretching from Colorado to Georgia. Our small population is diverse, and friendly. Friendly to the point everyone knows everyone else."

After the AAA Travel Guide description of Mexia, A.C. said, "Sounds like a great little town."

"Now, Mr. Mottola. We need to discuss your grandmother's estate."

"Estate? You sound like I'm walking into a fortune. I doubt if she had much?"

"She was well off," Miller said. "You are walking into a sizeable estate. Perhaps not by Californian standards. I valued the estate at a million."

"A million?" asked an astonished A.C. "As in a million dollars?"

"Your grandparents invested well. They owned property here in Limestone County."

"You mean the house, right?"

"Yes, there is the house. Then there are the thirty acres they leased to a rancher. He has expressed an interest in the property in the back. I am confident he would purchase the land should you decide to sell."

"I'm not a rancher, so yes, I'd be willing to sell. Is that all?"

"No. They own some commercial property around town. Most of the properties are generating income. This is prime commercial real estate and if you decide to sell, I should be able to get you a good price. But—"

"I knew it," said A.C., looking over his coffee. "There is always a but."

"There is this one property south of the town square. It is a cinder block building, and it is vacant. It has been empty for a while. She was paying someone to keep it from becoming an eyesore. Like many businesses, they left for the mall out on I-45."

"Any interest in that building?

"No. I could see if anyone's interested, but do not get your hopes up. They also had a stock portfolio."

After lunch, the two men reviewed the stock portfolio.

"The bulk of the estate is here," explained Miller. "Unless you need money, I would encourage leaving this alone. When you retire, it should provide a handsome retirement income. But that is up to you. Stan Shulman with A.G. Edwards is her broker. He is out of town this week. I told him you were on your way. He will be happy to meet with you, say on Monday."

"Works for me," said A.C.

Miller took A.C. around town and the county, pointing out his various real-estate holdings. Then he pulled up to the vacant building.

Miller parked along Slauson and they got out. It had been a variety of businesses. Walking to the front, Miller pointed. "There is street entrance here on Monrovia Street."

A. C. pointed to a large door. "What is that?"

"Can't say for sure. I don't remember if your grandparents installed it after they bought it, or if it was part of the original construction."

"Can we get inside?"

"Sorry." Miller checked the time, and he said he didn't bring the key with him. "I am running short on time. I need to meet another client this afternoon. OK if we look inside tomorrow morning?"

"No problem."

* * *

Back in his hotel room, A.C. let everything settle in. He realized California real estate was going through the roof and was not sure he could justify his storefront. A.C. saw a new opportunity with the vacant building.

Online streaming services had made CDs obsolete, and maintaining a storefront was expensive. This new building, already his, would allow him to restructure his business and improve his bottom line. He was sure the building had room for his inventory and an office for his online business. What he wanted was room to open a proper recording studio. A.C. enjoyed catering to local musicians.

Housing was not an issue. His grandmother's house was ideal for him, and only five minutes away.

After setting everything in everything in motion, A.C. accepted an offer from the rancher leasing his grandmother's ranch property. He then sold off the commercial property as well, leaving only his grandmother's house and the vacant building.

"About the vacant building," Miller said. "The interest is in the land only."

"That's OK. I am keeping the building."

"Are you sure?" asked Miller. "What are you thinking?"

"You know," A.C. said, "California is becoming very expensive. I have two months left on my store lease. My landlord let me know a significant rent increase is coming. I am considering closing rather than renewing the lease."

"Are you sure?"

"I wasn't until I came here."

"The vacant building?" Miller asked.

"The vacant building. Most of my business is online, and a storefront is not essential. With no lease or mortgage payments to consider, I can conduct my online business here. I can still have my storefront, and after our walk through, I am confident I can fit my recording studio there."

"Sounds like you've given this some thought."

"I may need some help, though." A.C. paused. "I got a copy of the building's plans from the county office and sent them to my architect in California. I will have him review them to see if the space can meet my needs."

"OK. Where do I come in? How can I help you?"

"I am going to need a contractor. Know any good ones?"

"I'm sure I can find you what you need."

"It will take me two or three weeks to close up shop. I will call when I'm heading back. Then you can set up a meeting with the contractors."

"Not a problem."

"Tomorrow, I head back to California. In a couple of days, I will call you and give you an update."

"I'll look forward to hearing from you."

CHAPTER 2

Before he left Texas, A.C. called Dean Torrence. A.C. and Dean played high school football and now Dean is his real-estate agent in Los Angeles.

"Torrence Real Estate," the voice said as they answered it.

"Dean?"

"A.C. Welcome back to So-Cal. How was Texas?"

A.C. took a deep breath before continuing. "I guess I didn't tell you."

"Tell me what?" asked Dean.

"The trip was not a vacation. My grandmother passed away, and I had to take care of things. I am her only grandchild and sole heir."

"Sorry to hear that. How are you holding up?"

A.C. took another deep breath before continuing, "I flew there with nothing on my mind except my grandmother. There was more there than expected."

"OK, I'll bite. What did you discover?"

"Quite a lot. Can we meet?" asked A.C.

"When will you get in?"

"Late tonight. Can we meet tomorrow?"

"Let me check my calendar. "I have a tour of new listings tomorrow morning and a Continuing Ed. class in the afternoon. I have two hours around lunch, or we can meet in my office at ten the following morning."

There was a pause as A.C. considered the options.

"Of course, if it is important, we can meet tomorrow evening. Whatever works for you."

"No, it isn't all that urgent. How about tomorrow morning in your office?"

"Great. I'll see you here at ten. I have nothing until a showing tomorrow afternoon. We will have time to catch up.

"Good. I'll see you then," and he hung up.

* * *

A.C. unpacked, checked his mail and phone messages. Nothing urgent awaited his attention. A quick burger at In-n-Out and then to the store. Then more mail and business messages greeted him. Again, nothing urgent. However, it was a different story when he opened his website. He had a half-dozen orders to fill. A.C. filled the orders and prepared them for shipping and dropped them off at the post office.

A.C. sat at his desk, eyes closed, and contemplated his new situation. Money was not a problem. He kept this to himself. His business was profitable, and he invested well. True, real-estate values were going sky high, but he was not concerned. He owned several rental properties and had his own stock portfolio. Even without his grandmother's inheritance, A.C. had a net worth in the millions.

A.C. described his store as a loss-leader. Store sales did not cover the rent, but he enjoyed having it and chatting with the occasional walk-in. A.C. believed the Texas deal offered exciting new challenges.

The ringing phone startled him back to reality.

"Mottola's Music," he said as he picked up the receiver.

The line was quiet for a second. Then an electronic voice began selling time-share opportunities. As soon as the voice started, A.C. hung up. He turned off the lights, locked the door, and headed home.

A.C. stopped for a quick meal at Marie's, a small family-style restaurant, and ordered the daily blue plate special. Today it was meatloaf, potatoes and lima beans. As he ate, A.C. made a list of things he needed to do.

When he arrived home, jet lag set in. His journey earlier had involved two hours getting to DFW, an hour getting through security, and a three-hour flight. Another ninety minutes getting from LAX to home. And that was before visiting the store. A.C. sat on the bed and turned on a news station. He need the noise to fill the silence of the room as he stared blankly at the screen. After a few minutes, he got up and took a quick shower then fell asleep as his head hit the pillow. The television turned itself off a few minutes later.

* * *

A.C. did not set his alarm, allowing his body to recuperate. He fixed himself a fried egg, toast, and coffee. Getting out his to-do list, he planned out his day.

"Butterfield and Associates," a woman said a few minutes later after A.C. had punched in the number.

"Paul Butterfield, please."

"Mr. Butterfield is with a client. May I take a message?"

"Just tell him Anthony Mottola called and have him call me back. He has my number."

"Yes, sir. I will give him the message." A.C. hung up. He got the plans for the vacant building and began making notes. Ten minutes later, Butterfield was on the line.

"Hi, Paul. Catch you at a bad time?" A.C. said.

"Nah. What's up? Heard you were in Texas," Paul said in a friendly tone. Paul was never a just-the-facts kind of guy.

"My grandmother passed away and I am her only heir."

"Sorry for your loss," Paul said.

"Thank you. What would you say if I moved to Texas?"

"I'd say you're crazier than I thought!" Paul let out a laugh. "Seriously, Anthony. What is going on?"

Paul and A.C. met through volunteering at the Salvation Army. A.C.'s name tag had said *Anthony* and Paul had called A.C. Anthony ever since.

"A new opportunity. My grandmother lived in a small town in Central Texas. She had some property, including a vacant building. I'm thinking about leaving the California rat race and moving to Texas."

Paul chuckled and said that he thought about leaving every day.

"One of my new properties is a vacant storefront. It offers more space than I have now, and it's rent free!" A.C. said.

"Sounds great. What do you need from me?"

"I have the plans from the county office. I want your suggestions of what I need to fix it up to meet my needs."

"Anthony, I can give you a starting point, but that is about all. I would feel better if I could see the building for myself. County plans are not always reliable."

"That's OK. I'll take your plans and give them to a local contractor. I just need a starting point. Can we meet and show you what I have?"

"Sure, always available for an Army friend," Paul said, referring to their volunteering at the Salvation Army.

"How about two this afternoon?" A.C. asked.

After a pause, the architect said, "Gotcha down, see you at two."

* * *

A.C. was five minutes early when he walked into Torrence Realty. Dean met him at the door and led the way to his office.

"OK, A.C. Spill the beans. What are you up to?" Dean asked.

"Dean, I am considering moving to Texas."

"What?"

"I inherited some property. One is a vacant storefront. It is ideal for what I do. Most of my business is online anyway, so my physical location is not important. The building provides more space than I have now."

"Sounds great."

"Dean, the building is mine. No rent."

They both laughed. "So, ole buddy, what can I do for you?"

"I have my home and three rental properties," said A.C.

Dean was watching his friend, noticing the excitement in A.C.'s voice and on his face. "You want to liquidate or be a long-distance owner. We can manage the properties for you."

"That's why I am here. I'm not sure what to do. You're the expert. What do you suggest?"

"Well," Dean started, his fingertips meeting, "I would recommend selling your personal residence. It is in an ideal location and should fetch a handsome price."

"And the rentals?" A.C. asked.

"Hold on to those for the moment. We can work out a management agreement. If I find interest in one or more, we can negotiate a sale then. If you put them on the market now as you are leaving for Texas, may signal trouble. You will lose a ton of money. You O.K. with cash?"

"Not a problem," assured A.C.

"Good. Then I suggest you hang on to them."

The two talked for another hour as A.C. explained about his grandmother, her estate, and the opportunities he found. Then they went for lunch.

* * *

A.C. spent some time at his store. He called and let the building owner he would not be renewing his lease. As he put down the phone, he realized even before the trip to Texas, he had considered moving. It was clear that time had come.

Paul Butterfield met A.C. as he walked into the Butterfield and Associates' office. It was an architectural and engineering firm started by Paul's father. Although Paul's father was still involved, Paul ran the business. Paul said, "You know, A.C. people are considering moving to Texas. It is getting crowded here in the Valley."

"When I made the trip, it never entered my mind that I might move. But…" A.C. did not finish. "Here are the plans." He unrolled them on a large table.

"What are you looking for?" asked Paul

"I want a small storefront, an office, and a shipping area. You know, I don't have a dedicated shipping area now. Is there room for that? I also need a recording studio. Similar to what I have now."

Butterfield responded, "Sounds ambitious. What is my timetable?"

"I'm heading back in two weeks. It would be nice, but not essential if I had them when I left."

"It will be tight, but doable," assured Paul.

They settled in Paul's office and got caught up on things. A.C. was Paul's best man at his wedding the year before.

Another busy day behind him, A.C. arrived home without going by his store. He ate takeout from Pei Wei's and relaxed with an episode of *Outlander*. A.C. looked at his list and only one more thing needed doing. He decided it could wait. Tomorrow, he would call Miller and bring him up to date. He got a beer from the fridge and lost himself in the television drama.

CHAPTER 3

A MONTH AFTER burying his grandmother, A.C. pulled his U-Haul up to his grandmother's house. His California house was on the market for forty-eight hours when he received an offer for more than the listed price. A.C. sold the furniture with the house.

The store was a different matter. A.C. hired a company to box up everything and ship it to Mexia. He found a new climate-controlled storage facility and rented three of the largest units. A.C. put his inventory in storage until he had renovated the vacant building on Monrovia Street. He sold his recording equipment. A new system sounded better than trying to ship the old studio.

The lease on his California store wasn't up for another month. A.C. paid the remaining time on his lease and gave the keys to Dean Torrence, who negotiated the sale of the studio contents. Once the store was empty, Dean would return the keys to the building owner.

"I know I told you to hold on to the rental properties," Dean said, "but a new real-estate management firm called looking for rental properties. They are offering more than the appraised value and moved ahead with the deal. I expect to have those sold within six months. Assuming that's OK with you."

"By all means. That is one less headache for me." A.C. looked forward to a fresh start. Dean was in the market for a new car and bought A.C.'s two-year-old BMW. Now, A.C. needed a car.

He called his new friend, Mitch Miller, for help. Three days after arriving in his new home state of Texas, Miller found him a year-old Suburban in Austin.

A.C. not only wanted a Suburban, but he also needed one. He loved his BMW, but the Suburban felt better suited to him and the open spaces of Texas. A.C. connected the dealer in Austin with his banker in California and paid cash for the car. Then A.C. followed Miller back to Mexia. He felt he was now at home.

A.C. had a new home, business, and car.

* * *

A.C. was the topic of conversation at the community services office as he changed the service from his grandmother to his name. At six foot four and just shy of two hundred and eighty pounds, A.C. had a thick, four-inch beard with a shaved head. He had owned motorcycles in the past but gave up riding after a good friend died following an accident.

His physique, however, had *biker* all over it. Then there was his voice. A.C.'s voice was not a typical biker voice. He was soft-spoken, articulate, and polite. You liked this man the first time you met him.

The plans of the vacant building Paul Butterfield sent him suggested a six-week renovation period. However, the business was up and running in less than five. The signage announced the new location of Mottola's Music and More. The locals abbreviated the name to *Triple M*. He gave away the new business cards to local merchants. Some of the local eateries allowed him to leave a few too. He mailed brochures to businesses offering his services to help with audio ads and voice-overs. High-schoolers with their own bands, as well as other musicians in the area, came in and cut custom CDs to sell at concerts.

A.C. could not be happier. Then he met Richard Skelton.

Richard was the antithesis of A.C. He was short, thin, and had a thick head of blonde hair.

"Excuse me, are you Anthony Mottola?" the stranger asked. A.C. was at a bin of old vinyl records.

"Yes, but most call me A.C." A.C. stopped to study him.

The stranger stretched out his hand, "Hi. I'm Richard Skelton. I answer to just about anything."

A.C. liked the man.

"I'm on my way home from Houston. I heard about your place. So, I thought I would check you out."

"What is your business? Need a jingle?" asked A.C.

"Nope. I'm in the same business as you. I'm out of Roanoke."

"You're a long way from Virginia," commented A.C.

"Not from Virginia. Roanoke is a little town north of Fort Worth. Ever hear of Texas Motor Speedway?"

"No," A.C. said. "I'm not much into racing."

"This little racetrack is on I-35 at 114. That's also the turnoff to Roanoke, where I have a little store on Oak Street. You need to come up some time."

"Maybe I will. So, what took you to Houston?"

"Record show. There are several major record and music shows in this five-state area, with Texas in the middle of it all."

The man surveyed the store's inventory. A.C. watched as he did so, then then the man asked, "You sell old vinyl?"

"Old and new plus CDs, DVDs. The market is growing for everything. Especially for those who want to handle what they buy. I see a lot of vinyl here. This is all you do?"

"It keeps me busy. I also sell rare entertainment memorabilia through my online store."

"I'll have to check you out."

A.C. pointed to his office. "Over here. I'll show you my site." Richard stood behind A.C. as the computer came alive and A.C.'s webpage appeared on the screen. He took his new friend on a tour of the site, pointing out some valuable stock.

"A.C., listen. A friend of mine is starting a new music festival in Luckenbach. It is a small town. About two hours southwest of here. The festival is being run by a board of directors. A group of vendors with the type of merchandise to draw an audience. This will be a premiere festival. Interested? I believe I can get you in on the ground floor."

"Ground floor?" A.C. asked. A telltale smile was on his face.

"This means you get to pick your spot. In the center of the action. This will be your permanent spot. You also will have a seat on the board of directors and help guide the festival along."

"Sounds expensive. What does this seat on the board set me back?"

"Five grand, which is our initial working capital. To cover our immediate expenses, vendors are charged ten percent of sales. Board members are charged only five percent. This covers the cost of renting the facility, utilities, security, and insurance. We also charge a nominal fee for the space. This ensures we don't over-sell the spaces."

"And board members?" asked A.C.

"Your space is yours. You may sell it to another seller or include it in your estate." Skelton paused, waiting for another question. "Tell you what, A.C., give me a business card and I will send the paperwork to you. If you're interested, call and I'll reserve a spot for you. We can do the paperwork then."

"What if I sign up but then decide the festival isn't for me?" A.C. asked.

"Simple. We'll advertise your spot; keep. We keep ten percent, and you get the rest. There are no guarantees you'll get your money back. I'd be surprised if you didn't make a profit. There are a few spaces left and a high demand for them. Right now, these are by invitation only."

"And I am invited?"

"Yes."

A.C. opened a drawer and pulled out his checkbook. "I'm in. I can give you a check today if that's OK with you."

"Works for me," said Skelton.

"Great. Here is $500 as a deposit. Or do you need more?"

"No, the five hundred deposit will suffice. I will email you the forms and you can send the balance when you send back the forms. Here's my card. Let me know if you have questions."

A.C. pointed to a vacant chair. "Got time to relax?"

"Always nice to break up the ride from Houston."

A.C. opened a mini-fridge and pulled out two bottles of Shiner Bock. Holding out a bottle to his visitor, he sat behind his desk. "Good beer. Just discovered this." He raised his bottle in a toast and the two sat and shared stories.

That night, A.C. and Johnnie Walker celebrated his new venture. Taking a sip of the Scotch, A.C. opened his computer and reviewed what Skelton sent him. He checked out the festival's web page and recognized some of the directors. Satisfied with what he read, A.C. completed the online forms, added his credit card information, and hit send. He closed his computer satisfied he had made the right decision.

* * *

Jacques Dutronc was sitting at a sidewalk café watching the people go by. No one paid attention to the small pack of cigarettes he had aimed at the table next to him. There, Ross Bagdesarian and Alan Bergman were engaged in quiet conversation. Lucio Dalla seated himself at the next table over, watching people as well. Neither Dutronc nor Lucio cared about the pedestrian traffic. Dutronc's pack of cigarettes recorded the conversation between Bagdesarian and Bergman. Lucio was looking for signs of trouble.

Bagdesarian was part of a new crime family. Some people called these families the mob, the mafia or the Cosa Nostra. Bagdesarian and Dutronc simply referred to them as *the family.* Bergman was a new face. Dutronc was unsure how Bergman fitted into the family. Perhaps he was not in the family. Interpol knew Bagdesarian, as did the French and Italian police. Interpol assigned Investigator Dutronc to bring Bagdesarian and his new family down.

Lucio was old school. He was born and raised in Palermo, a city on the western side of Sicily. He worked for several old families before going rogue. Becoming a gun-for-hire. Bagdesarian made him, Dalla, *an offer he could not refuse.* Now, Lucio was Bagdesarian's bodyguard.

Dutronc, who had been with Interpol for less than a year, was unknown to Lucio. However, Dutronc understood Lucio and his loyalties, which is why the cigarette case monitored Bagdesarian. Watching the pedestrian traffic kept everyone in his line of sight. This meant he could listen in on Bagdesarian's conversation and keep a watchful eye on Lucio as he pretended to read his paper.

* * *

Etienne's is a new oyster bar in New Orleans's French Quarter. Alan Bergman and Ross Bagdesarian were seated at a secluded table. Lucio Dalla was at a separate table where he could observe the surroundings.

"Here is the deposit," said Bagdesarian as he handed Bergman a large envelope. The envelope contained several bundles of $100 bills. Bergman examined the contents, then smiled after putting it on the table.

"I head to St. Thomas in the morning," said Bergman. Bagdesarian believed these cash deposits made it difficult for authorities to track. "Two days later it will be in our special account in the Caymans."

"Anyone looking at that account?" Bagdesarian asked.

"No one yet."

"Good," Bagdesarian said with satisfaction. "In time, they will. Right now, let's just keep it under their radar."

"Couldn't agree more," said a smiling Bergman.

"Any thoughts on what business to open?"

"I've looked at a few. A friend of mine has been buying rare vinyl albums."

"Vinyl?" asked Bagdesarian.

"Vinyl. You know. Big, black round disks. You put a needle in the groove, and it plays music."

"My grandmother had a record player, I think." Bagdesarian paused, looked at Lucio, who ignored him. This was the pre-arranged sign there were no problems. "So, why is this of interest?"

"A lot of sales are online and difficult to trace. A perfect business to buy."

"Or take over," Bagdesarian said.

"Yeah, whatever. Anyway, getting into that business means we buy and sell this old stuff. It would be ideal for us to launder your money."

"Think it will work?" asked Bagdesarian.

"I found a couple of businesses in Texas with physical stores, plus an online presence. I will get to know them and how the business works. If it is plausible, I will get back to you."

"How long?" asked Bagdesarian.

A puzzled Bergman asked, "How long what?"

"You know. How long before I hear something?"

"Can't say for sure. I will check in on even-numbered Fridays and bring you up to date. And if I found a target. OK with you?"

"I like the even-numbered date thing. Better than every-other Friday crap. Unless we have something."

"Good. After I make the deposit in the Caymans, I will fly to Texas."

"Where will you start?" asked Bagdesarian.

"Start in the center, Austin, I think. They bill it as the music capital of Texas."

"Let's break it up." With a nod toward Dutronc, "That guy has been there a long time. His cigarette case is on the table. Yet, he hasn't smoked since we've been here. I'll have Lucio check him out."

"Good. You go now," suggested Bergman. "I will watch him. If he heads off in the same direction, I'll text you. If he follows me, no problem. I hope he likes the cinema."

No formalities. Just the end to a conversation. Bagdesarian left and a minute later, Lucio followed. The cigarette man remained in place. Bergman left, heading in a different direction. He stopped at several store windows where he could observe the café's reflection in the window. The cigarette man was still there, watching people and reading his paper.

Bergman sent a text to Bagdesarian. *Still there, no movement.* Bergman turned the corner and was gone.

CHAPTER 4

A silver Lexus GX pulled up in front of the nondescript building. At one time, the building had been a 7-Eleven convenience store, then a liquor store. Today, it housed *Alan Bergman Music.* The driver got out first. He was a short, stocky man in jeans, a white shirt but no tie, and a blue blazer. His mirrored sunglasses reflected the store in their lenses. He glanced in both directions before opening the door for his passenger. At six foot three, the passenger towered over his driver. Dressed in a tan suit and tie-less white shirt, he stepped onto the sidewalk, nodded toward the store's entrance, and followed his driver. A sign with gold-foil letters adorned the door, announcing ABM, with music quarter notes on each side. As they entered the building, a buzzer announced their arrival.

Alan Bergman, expecting the visitors, was in his office. He was in the doorway watching them. "Welcome. Have any trouble finding the place?" He stepped behind the duo, slit the door sign from open to closed and then locked the door. ABM was shut.

"Trouble. You should name this place Black Hole, not Black Hollow. Lucio, here," said the tall man, pointing to his driver, "got lost three times."

With raised eyebrows, Bergman asked the driver, "You got lost? Three times?"

Lucio did not acknowledge the question. Instead, his eyes hidden behind sunglasses, Lucio continued to survey the store's interior.

Bergman looked for a signal from Bagdesarian but saw none. Turning back to Lucio. "I thought I gave you pretty explicit instructions." Bergman suppressed a smile and asked again, "Three times?"

Lucio responded with a facial expression that said, *"Don't ask me again unless you want those to be your last words."*

Bergman pointed a thumb in Lucio's direction and asked, "Does he ever talk?"

"When he talks," deadpanned Bagdesarian, "People die."

Bergman cleared his throat. "Isn't this perfect? Good internet is all I need. It is off the beaten path, and I get a few customers daily. Most of the business, however, is online. Here," Bergman said, handing him a vinyl single, "I just sold this for five-and-a-quarter."

"I hope you get more than five bucks and change per sale," Bagdesarian replied.

"No, not $5.25. That record just sold for $525.00." Then, retrieving the record, Bergman read the label, "'The Witch Doctor' by David Seville."

Bagdesarian said, "Never heard of either." They were not interested in the inventory.

A few beads of sweat appeared on Bergman's forehead, and he added quickly, "Seville made a fortune with three singing chipmunks, but this was his first big hit. Very few pristine copies exist today."

"What's our profit?"

"$500. I bought it at an estate sale where the appraiser didn't know what he had. So, I bought a box of similar-condition singles."

"You said you had something big coming up."

Bergman handed the record to his guest. "There is a lot of money in record shows. That record in your hands is new—only two years old. It has attracted a huge following, and I have secured a spot at the next show."

"And this is the big news?"

"No. But Anthony Mottola is the number one seller of this stuff in the area. He will be there. Maybe for the last time."

"What? Are you going to take him out?"

"No need to. A higher authority has intervened." Bergman pointed to the ceiling. "Goes by A.C., and the guy seems to have some health concerns. Word is the angels," making an upward gesture, "want him up there."

"Going to buy him out?"

"That's my intent. First, I need to meet A.C. and win his confidence. Then I need to confirm the rumors. Then I can approach him with an offer to buy him out. It all depends on how serious his illness is."

Bagdesarian gave Bergman a suspicious look over the top of his glasses, "What if he won't sell?"

"I can be very persuasive," Bergman said. He was smiling and hoping to sound and appear confident.

"It's been over two years since you landed in this forsaken part of America. We made a significant investment in you. We can't have a Black Hole here suck up all that cash. Capisce?"

"Got it under control."

Lucio stood guard at the door as Bergman and Bagdesarian wandered through the store. "Any wiggle room in this business?" asked Bagdesarian.

"Always wiggle room," answered Bergman. But, of course, he knew wiggle room was code for counterfeit items.

"Just so we understand one another."

"No problem there," Bergman assured Bagdesarian.

Pointing to Lucio, "Are you sure he can talk?"

"Want him to say something?"

"Sure, why not?"

"He will have to kill you."

Bergman let out an embarrassed laugh. "In that case, I'll pass."

"Alan, my boy. That was not a joke."

Bagdesarian signaled Lucio to remain in the store as he and Bergman entered the office. Bagdesarian closed the door behind him. "I need you to understand the money I gave you was not mine. It came from some very cautious investors."

"Bergman nodded to show he understood."

"The investors expect a significant return on their investment."

Bergman was silent.

"These investors won't be happy with anything less. Their disappointment can be very painful, and I am not limiting it to money. Are we clear?"

"Yes, Ross, I won't let anybody down.

Satisfied that Bergman understood what he was saying, Bagdesarian ended the meeting. The two were laughing and joking as they exited the office. Bergman walked over and unlocked the door. He watched his two visitors enter their rented Lexus and drive off. As he closed the door, his cell phone rang. It was Bagdesarian.

"You got six months. Otherwise, I will end our agreement. Permanently!"

The phone went dead. Bergman stood and looked at it.

* * *

The opening door jingled the bell twice. It jingled again when it closed.

"Be right with you."

"Take your time. I'm in no rush," the customer replied.

A.C. came from the storage area behind his office. His mood lightened when he saw the visitor.

"Ragsdale! Is that you? I can't believe my eyes."

"In the flesh, as they say."

With their hands clasped, they gave each other a one-armed hug, pounding each other's back. "What in the world brings you to these parts?" A.C. asked before letting go.

"You do," Ragsdale said.

"Me?" said a surprised A.C.

"You sent me a cryptic email last week. Said you w
ere sick and thinking of retiring. So, I came running to my old friend to see how I could help."

"Thanks, but there's not a lot you can do. Not health-wise, at any rate."

"So, I wasted my time flying back here. You realize I needed a divining rod to find your place in the middle of nowhere."

"Old friends sharing time isn't a waste of time. And this is not nowhere. It is the suburbs of somewhere!"

Ragsdale laughed and shook his head.

The two sat in the office with the door closed and reminiscing their shared experiences. "It's been what? Two, three years? Since we last saw each other?"

Ragsdale laughed and shook his head. "Four. We last saw each other at Normandy, celebrating the anniversary of D-Day."

A.C. said, "Hard to believe it's been that long. Say, if you have time, let's head to Waco and grab dinner. It's a slow day. Give me a few minutes to lock up."

"I do have one question," Ragsdale said as he stood up and stretched. "Any place to stay around here? I'm beat and need a place to crash."

"There is a five-star hotel is right outside of town. Best of all, it's free!"

"Ah, A.C. I can't impose on you. You didn't even know I was coming."

"Pooh," A.C. said as he turned the key and locked his store. "It may not be as fancy or as highfalutin as the Roosevelt back home. But it is clean. Besides, we can catch up on the real reason you are here. I even have some Jack Daniels truth serum."

"OK, OK." Then, in mock seriousness, Ragsdale asked, "You drive a car or a horse and buggy?"

"You know dang well I sold that buckboard. To you, no less!" They were enjoying the banter. "No, I am in the twenty-first century. I even have an actual gas-guzzling automobile." They walked around the side where waiting was a gold, vintage 1969 Cadillac Eldorado sitting next to a dark blue Chevy Suburban.

"When did you get this?" Ragsdale said, admiring the metallic gold auto, running his hand along the front quarter panel.

"Found it a while back. At an auto auction in Austin. It wasn't going for as high as I thought it would. Turns out it was even less if I paid cash. Ain't it a beaut?"

They got in, and the car roared to life. The two old friends headed west.

"Where are we heading?"

"New place. I discovered it in downtown Waco. Owner is Pete Drake, a new friend. *Pete's Place* is a carnivore's delight. It has steak, ribs, and since this is Friday, prime rib to die for."

"Sounds like heaven," Ragsdale said, admiring his friend's set of wheels.

"Wait till you taste the meat. After all, this is Texas!" A.C. was smiling, with his eyes glued to the road ahead.

They sat in a booth as A.C. introduced Ragsdale to Pete. After introductions and a few jokes, they ordered the prime rib dinner. It arrived with grated horseradish, a loaded baked potato, and a side salad.

Pete brought over two steins of IPA. "Local brew," Pete said. "There are a couple of boutique breweries in the area. This," holding up the steins, "is my favorite."

"What's it called?" asked A.C.

Standing straight and with a note of austerity, Pete said, "Mammoth IPA." Everyone laughed. "Named after the dinosaur dig out near our airport." They shared a few more stories, then Pete left the friends to enjoy their dinner.

CHAPTER 5

"So, WHAT IS on your mind?" Ragsdale took another bite of his prime rib and studied his friend.

A.C. watched his buddy for a few seconds before responding. "Look, you've talked about leaving California and getting some land. You said getting a horse and doing some riding was your dream retirement. At least, that is how I recall it. You know, at your place in California."

"Yeah," he said, taking a swig of his Mammoth Ale.

"Is it still your dream?"

Ragsdale looked at his friend over his tankard

"Is it still your dream to have the ranch, the horses? The whole nine yards?" A.C. asked.

"Sure. But where to start?"

"Ann Tweedy is a realtor friend and buys a lot of stuff from me. We have talked about you in a roundabout way. Two hours west is the little village of Erwindale. She has a ranch with ten acres for sale. It includes a magnificent house."

Ragsdale said with a wide grin, "Better 'n yours?"

A.C. chuckled at the comment. "No, but I am sure it will meet your mediocre expectations!" A.C. lifted his glass of ale in a mock toast, then added. "There is a barn which looks much like the one Owen used to use."

"You mean Bradley? In Nashville?"

"Yeah, that's the one." A.C. continued, "The barn now houses farm implements. With a bit of effort, however, you could turn it into one heck of a recording studio. Bigger and better than what I have. Probably better than anything else in Texas."

"Worried about me taking business away from you?"

"Nah. You know, some locals use my facility for making demos. My studio is small, and my overhead is low. So it costs me next to nothing to help them record. No. Most of my clients could not afford what you offer. Besides, they are local."

"And mine?" asked Ragsdale.

"Your facility would attract larger and established acts," said A.C. "They'd come for the same reason they went to Owen. Or down to Muscle Shoals. Your facility would have a unique sound. Everyone is looking for the new sound that will set them apart." A.C. and Ragsdale were quiet for several sends. Then, A.C. added, "You could add a film studio. You could film documentaries and commercials and edit larger projects."

"OK. Let's say I am interested. How much?"

"Just over two." A.C. waited for a reaction.

"Two? Two what."

"Million. Two million."

"I sure hope it includes running water, and I don't mean a stream for a bathroom!"

"Hey, old buddy, remember this is Texas, not California. The price is a third of what you'd pay out there." Then, seeing Ragsdale's expression, A.C. added, "And you'd get less than half the land you're getting here."

"Why would I move to Texas?"

"I can think of three things right off the top. First, there is none of that state income tax stuff in Texas. That's all you complained about the last time I was with you."

"You got that right," Ragsdale said, leaning back in his chair.

"Second, I don't know if you noticed the sky when you came in today? It was blue, not brown, and you didn't have to chew it as you took a deep breath."

"OK, so far, so good. What's the third?"

"We get to hang out more. What could be better than that?"

"You should have started with that one. Call your real-estate friend and set it up."

"Already done. When you were in the little boy's room, I talked to Ann. She will meet us tomorrow afternoon. Sometime around two."

"You sure like the number two, don't you?"

"Beats the devil out of one—or none. Which is closing in on me."

A.C. drove Ragsdale around Waco, pointing out various sights and attractions before heading back to Mexia.

As they rolled into town, Ragsdale asked, "Where is everybody?"

"They roll the sidewalks up at dusk."

They were in a good mood as they pulled into A.C.'s drive.

* * *

Ragsdale picked A.C. up at his house in a slate-gray Bronco he rented at the airport.

"That the best you can do?" chided A.C.

"It ain't no 'Dorado, but it will have to do in a pinch." Ragsdale was having difficulty getting the truck into gear. "Blasted. I am still trying to get used to this dial to change gears. I'm afraid I'll put it in reverse when I mean drive." Both men laughed.

"Remember the Edsel and push buttons?" A.C. teased.

"Don't remind me. My dad had one, and that's what I drove for my driver's license!" After getting the truck into gear, he asked, "So. Where am I going?"

"This is U.S. 84. Just keep heading west until we'll reach 183. Then we will turn and head north. But right now, just sit back. Don't touch that dial. In the words of Eddie Kendricks, just keep on a truckin'." A.C. sat back to enjoy the ride.

"You know. You could make it more adventurous with a

turn or two."

"Could have, but I've ridden with you. I know how easily you get lost. Remember when we went to that record show, up Topanga Canyon?" A.C. said, laughing, "that was an adventure."

"It was a straight shot, up Topanga."

A.C. turned to look at his friend and said, "Straight? There is nothing straight about that road."

"Yes but turning down Starlight should have been a clue. Instead, it took two hours to turn around. And then we wound up late to the show."

"But we made it." A.C. said ending the memory.

They drove through the small town of Pear. One caution light, two churches, and a Mexican restaurant. They stopped, stretched, and got a bite to eat. The restaurant was a small mom-and-pop venture. It used to be a house. The restaurant used two bedrooms, a dining room, and a living room. A.C. and Ragsdale were seated in a converted bedroom with two tables. One table had a family of four, while they found themselves at a window.

"Tamales are good," A.C. said, setting his menu aside.

"You've been here before," Ragsdale said. This was more of a statement than a question.

"You could say that."

"We splitting a dozen, or are you going to scoff them all down yourself?" Ragsdale asked, also setting his menu aside.

"I guess I can cut back and share them."

"How big of you."

The waitress came and took their order. A few minutes later, she returned with two long-neck Coronas and a lime wedge in each bottle's opening. They spent the time waiting by recalling previous experiences in California, New Mexico, and their one trip to Montana.

"We were stupid on that trip."

"It was eighty-five degrees in Los Angeles when we left. Who would have expected?"

"I guess our friends who tried to talk us out of it."

"Who ever heard of a blizzard in May?"

Laughing, Ragsdale said, "They told us it was a freak storm."

"True, or did they consider us freaks rolling into town in a convertible? With the top down, no less. It was a balmy forty-four degrees in the sun with a thirty-mile wind from the north!

"Over eight inches fell that night."

"At least I had the sense to put the top up!"

"Yeah, I'll give you that. But not until after it started snowing. Last time I'm going with you without checking the weather before we leave."

"But they were nice jackets, warm and rugged. Still own yours?" A.C. asked.

"Hanging in the closet next to the wet suit you insisted we buy in Bermuda."

"I try to forget that adventure. And that shack!"

Ignoring the comment, Ragsdale asked, "What about you? Still wear your jacket?"

"Nope. Got rid of them and a lot more when I moved to Texas."

"Why'd you move to the boonies in Texas?"

"My daughter. She's a veterinarian and went to Texas A&M. She liked her mom in Texas, but not too close. She was always closer to her mom and now…" A.C. never finished the thought. Ragsdale was quiet for a moment when A.C. picked up the story.

"My grandmother lived in Mexia. I was her only grandson and her sole heir. When she passed, I saw an opportunity to be close and keep an eye on her."

"I'm sorry, A.C. I don't know what to say."

"Forget it. I love my little house and it has lots of elbow room. I have learned to ride a horse and enjoy rodeos. There are friendly folks out here who don't base their friendship on anything other than who you are. In LA, you make and lose friendships based on your current last success or failure. Here, you are a friend until you prove you are not."

Back on the road, they traded more war stories.

"Here's your turn," said A.C., and Ragsdale slowed and made his turn.

"Two roads up, you will see a road called Thirsty Mule on the left."

Five minutes later, Ragsdale hit the brakes as he almost missed the turn. "Son, we have different ideas of what a road is." Ragsdale sat a minute and gazed at the dirt path his friend had called a road.

Laughing so hard, A.C. had a hard time talking, "Now you know why I had you drive this horse. I wasn't about to destroy my vintage ride torn up along this dirt trail."

"There was that Suburban."

"Just washed it and didn't want to get it dirty. Water shortage, you know." A.C. chuckled.

They reached the ranch two minutes later. A white wood fence extended two hundred feet on either side of a stone entrance arching over the drive with CHEYENNE welded in place. Ragsdale used a keypad to open the gate. Ahead was a large stone house with a white F-250 with oversized wheels sitting in front. Ragsdale pulled alongside as a woman in jeans, a Western hat, and cowboy boots hopped down from the truck's cab.

"There's Ann," A.C. said, before making the introductions as the three gathered at the Bronco's grill.

"Ten point five acres, the main house, and two outbuildings," said Ann. "There is the barn," she continued, pointing, then nodding to the second building, "that will accommodate up to ten horses. You ride?"

"A little. Hope to do a lot more," Ragsdale said, taking in the surroundings. "What about water?"

"There is a well near the house. However, some don't like the taste of well water and use a water cooler with twenty-gallon jugs for cooking and drinking. There is also a tank outback."

"Tank?" Ragsdale gave his friend a quizzical look. "Why do I need an Abrams?"

"'Pond' to you California sissies." She gave Ragsdale a slap on the back.

Turning to the realtor, Ragsdale said, "A.C. assures me it's a steal at 2.5 mil. I'm not so sure."

"A.C. tends to exaggerate."

Looking at his friend, "Exaggerating what? The value or the price?"

"Price," Ann responded. "It's been on the market for some time. The family patriarch owned the ranch. He has Alzheimer's, and now the family needs to sell."

"Family doesn't want it?"

"Yes and no. One son has a smaller ranch on the other side of 84; the rest are city folk. It's been in the family for generations and has sentimental value. But some of the sons don't even live in Texas anymore. So I tried to tell them that 2.5 was a little high. Finally, after six months, they listened and lowered the price. Today the asking price is 1.95, and that is a steal." She had a pleasant laugh that softened the mood.

"Let's tour the buildings and see if this is what you want," Ann said, gesturing for the men to follow "If not, I may have some other options. But I will be honest with you. The others may be less expensive, but they won't compare to what you will get with Cheyenne."

Surprised to get phone service, Ragsdale called his accountant in Pomona, and an hour later, Ragsdale made an offer on Cheyenne. He then called his lawyer and let him know of the offer.

They stopped at *Pete's Place* on their way to A.C.'s. Ragsdale ordered a large T-Bone steak for each of them. They celebrated Ragsdale's decision.

"What's the next step? Asked A.C.

"It will take a month or two, I guess. I will leave it up to my lawyer and accountant to work out the details. The accountant will make sure I don't overspend. The lawyer will make sure everything is as it should be.

###

"Can't stay any longer?" A.C. asked as Ragsdale loaded up his rented Bronco.

"No. I need to get the ball rolling. I can't afford homes in Texas and California. I'm not wealthy like you. I've got to take care of business and make my move to Cheyenne.

Your realtor friend is sending me the specs on the house and barn. I want to talk with an architect. I need a cost estimate for a few upgrades to the house. And for converting the barn to a recording studio."

"When will you be back?"

"Shouldn't take more than a month. Then we need to talk about your other problem."

"I'll be here. Just let me know when you're heading back."

"10-4 old, buddy." They hugged for a long moment. Then Ragsdale climbed into the Bronco, fired it up, and backed out of the drive.

A.C. stood and watched as his friend drove out of sight.

CHAPTER 6

A.C. WAS IN his office answering emails when he heard someone come into the store. "Be right with you," he yelled.

"No hurry, just browsing," the customer said.

A.C. finished emailing order information, closed the computer, and entered the store. He saw a man at the back of the shop. The man had a full head of hair. He wore jeans and a bright blue polo shirt and rimless glasses. He also sported a handlebar mustache. The man was several inches shorter than A.C., but so were most of the people he met. A.C. walked to the man, who was flipping through a box of albums.

"Welcome. Are you looking at anything in particular?"

"Mr. Mottola?" the man asked.

"Yes, but most folks call me A.C. Have we met?"

The man offered his hand and introduced himself. "I am Alan Bergman." The two shook hands. The stranger said, "I have a similar operation down in Black Hollow."

"Black Hollow? I'm not sure where that is."

The stranger laughed. "You're not the only one. Most people don't know it's only thirty miles away. South and east."

"Well, good for you. I didn't know anyone down there had a business."

"Online only. I don't have a storefront, so most of my stuff is in climate-controlled storage."

"How is your business doing?" A.C. asked, attempting to be polite.

Bergman pointed to a poster on the wall. "The Beatles at the Hollywood Bowl. Is that real or a replica?"

"At fifteen hundred, it better be real. I don't deal in knockoffs or replicas."

"But how can you be sure it is real?" Alan asked.

"Provenance. I know where the poster was before me. I provide a certificate of authenticity and a money-back guarantee if it turns out the provenance is wrong."

"Where did you get it?"

"Come on, Mr. Bergman. I can't reveal my sources. You can take it to the bank. If I sell you a poster, it is real. It came from a trusted stagehand, promoter or performer."

Bergman started walking around the store, studying the posters, awards, and pictures on the walls. "Want me to show you around?" asked A.C. He gave Alan a tour of Triple M while they talked. As they reached their starting point, Alan checked his watch.

"Mr. Bergman. Be honest with me. Why are you here? You have looked around, but you have bought nothing. In fact, nothing you saw seemed to pique your interest."

Looking at his watch again, Bergman replied, "As I said, just curious. I wanted to get a feel for your store. I wanted to get some ideas for my store down in Black Hollow. Look, Mr. Mottola."

"A.C. Please."

"Look, A.C. I was on my way to another appointment. Mexia is on the way, so I thought I'd stop. You know, just trying to be friendly. It was a pleasure meeting you and seeing your store. But I gotta go or be late for my appointment."

The two shook hands. A.C. stood at the door, watching as Bergman drove off. The whole deal bothered A.C. but he could not put a finger on it. After his visitor was out of sight, A.C. shrugged, closed the door and returned to work.

* * *

It was a quiet day in Mexia, and no one had come in all day. In the afternoon, as he was rummaging through various bins, filling online orders, the sound of the door opening and closing caught his attention.

A.C. looked up and recognized the visitor. "Alan Bergman, right?"

"Excellent memory," said Alan and offered his hand.

"Short-term is OK. You were in here a week or two back, right?" A.C.'s previous experience with this guy made him wary.

"Closer to four, but who is counting?" answered Alan.

"Well, what brings you back? In the market for some merchandise to stock your storage unit?"

"You might say that." Alan smiled.

There was something about that smile. It wasn't menacing, but it did not feel genuine either. A.C. was cordial and suspicious at the same time. He walked to his office and placed the records he held on a table. A.C.'s inner voice kept repeating. *Find out what he wants.* He picked up a stack of lobby cards and went to show them to Alan. "Let me show you what came in yesterday." He handed Alan a stack of 11X14 lobby cards.

"What are these? I don't know that I've ever seen them before."

"They're lobby cards," A.C. explained. "In the old days, when theaters housed a single screen, they also ran double features for a single price. So they hung these cards in the lobby to entice the customer to stay. But, of course, staying meant more concessions, which is where they made their money. Theaters would hang these like photographs." He picked out one card. "This is a lobby card for *The Ten Commandments,* starring Charlton Heston, depicting Moses parting the Red Sea."

"Is that true? They showed two movies for the price of one?"

"Some did, but all movies were continuous showings. You came in after the movie started, and you stayed until you got to that scene again. Hitchcock and *Psycho* changed all that. Hitchcock insisted theaters not allow anyone in after the first ten minutes of his thriller."

A.C. then picked out a lobby card for Bobby Darin. "Nightclubs had the same problem, only more so. Nightclub performers did not rely on large posters; they relied heavily on these lobby cards instead. These cards were hung to advertise acts coming to town. This one is for Bobby Darin at the Copa."

"Wow!" said Alan.

"They also used lobby cards in advertising. The large posters were full-page ads. Lobby cards were quarter-page ads. They were often more effective in drawing an audience than a single picture."

"How do you find these things?"

"Connections, my boy. Connections. These came from Gene Weed. I first met Gene when he was a hot D.J. for KFWB in Los Angeles. He later became a record and television producer. I got these after he retired. Someone found them in a vault. They put the word out. I got on the horn and made an offer. Voila, here they are."

His curiosity piqued, Alan asked, "Are they valuable?"

"It's a question of supply and demand. Also, who and what is being promoted. No one has used lobby cards in over three decades. Reproductions are rare and easy to identify. Most reproductions out there are on lighter card stock and the pictures are not as clear."

"How much is this Darin card?"

"This card will go for a hundred or two. But Darin signed this one for Gene. Now the value jumps two or three times."

"Wow," said Alan, and flipped through several cards.

"Like Sinatra, Darin did not have to rely on lobby cards to draw an audience, so there aren't many of their cards out there. And, like Sinatra, Darin did not autograph many items. So this is a rare find." A.C. studied his visitor for a long minute. "But," taking back the lobby cards. "You didn't come to look at these, did you?"

Alan handed the cards back to A.C. "No, you said something

about needing to expand your inventory," A.C. continued.

"Yeah. Well, I may have a way benefiting both of us."

A.C. looked at Bergman over his eyebrows. With some reluctance, he asked, "Both of us?"

"Simple. Word on the street is you may not be well. Cancer or something."

Raising his hand in a stop gesture, A.C. exclaimed, "Whoa there, cowboy. I don't know where you are getting your information, but you are walking through some dangerous territory here. I don't discuss my health with just anyone. Not with friends. And most of all, not with strangers. Where in the world did you come up with this preposterous notion?"

"From Bob Braun. Over in Oglesby."

"Bobby? You talked to Bobby Braun? Did he tell you I had cancer? That I was knocking on death's door?" A.C. stood there, almost daring his visitor to say something.

"Well," Bergman started with hesitation. "Not exactly."

"Well, what exactly did he say?" asked A.C., staring down his customer.

"There was an estate sale in Oglesby. It included a comprehensive record, CD, and DVD collection. I was there hoping to purchase the lot. I was late and Braun beat me to the punch. He purchased the lot himself."

"Good for him. But how does that translate to my dying of cancer?"

"We talked for a few minutes, and I congratulated him on the purchase."

"That was big of you.""That's how I got to know who he was."

"You still haven't answered my question."

"Hang on, I'm getting there. Braun was talking to Leslie Towns, the agent handling the estate sale. I heard your name come up in their conversation. I got a little closer to eavesdrop. That's when I heard Towns tell Braun he was concerned, since you had lost a lot of weight. He also noticed you seemed a little slower."

"So, you decided I was dying of cancer?" A.C. had put the cards down, folded his arms, and stared at Bergman.

"No, not me. At least, not at first."

"So, how did you come up with this wild diagnosis?"

"I don't remember how it came up. I overheard Braun saying he had a brother who died cancer. Braun said one of the disease's first signs was an unexplained weight loss."

"So I go on a diet. I drop a few pounds, and now I have cancer?"

"No, but Towns said he remembered you were once a heavy smoker. He speculated you might have lung cancer. I guess they both believed it."

"Are you buying any merchandise today?" asked A.C.

"No, I just—"

A.C. cut him off. "I think you should leave. I have orders to fill and my mood… Let's just say it is not congenial right now."

Bergman shrugged his shoulders. "I'll leave. Sorry to have upset you." He offered his hand, but A.C. turned his back on him and resumed pulling the merchandise. Then, hearing the door open and close, he watched Bergman get into his car and pull away. A.C. then locked the door, changed the sign to closed, and went to his office. After that, he decided that he and Jack Daniels needed to have a private conversation.

* * *

A.C. turned the store lights out, went back to his office, and closed the door. He sat at his desk with his eyes closed. He willed his blood pressure to drop and his breathing to calm down and poured two fingers of his buddy Jack, leaned back in his chair and closed his eyes. Then, when he was more relaxed, A.C. picked up his cell phone and dialed a number.

Bobby Braun felt his phone buzz in his pocket. Without looking at the caller's I.D., he swiped the screen with his thumb and answered with a single word. "Braun."

"Anthony Mottola."

"A.C.," said Braun. "How's it going?"

At the sound of Braun's voice, A.C.'s blood pressure rose and he blurted out more forcefully than intended, "You, tell me. You seem to know it all."

A.C. surprised Braun with his tone. Braun responded with hesitation and asked, "A.C.? Are you alright?" A.C. did not answer, so Braun continued, "I don't have—" A.C. cut him off. "Ever meet Alan Bergman?"

"Not that I recall," said Braun.

"Short guy, blonde hair, handlebar mustache. Was at the sale in Oglesby."

"Oh, that idiot. I don't think we said ten words to each other. Why?"

Ignoring the question, A.C. asked, "Who else did you talk to? After you talked to Bergman."

"Conrad Martindale. Again, why?"

"Not Towns?"

"What? No, not after I made my purchase. I hadn't seen Martindale in a month or two. We talked and got caught up. Why? What's the matter?"

"Did you tell Conrad I had cancer?"

"No. Where is this coming from?"

"Bergman said you did."

"We both noticed you seem thinner."

"And slower," added A.C.

"What? No. We commented on your weight loss and didn't remember you saying

anything about a diet. Martindale knew you were once a heavy smoker and hoped you did not have lung cancer. That's all."

"Your brother had lung cancer, right?"

"Brother-in-law. Died from it last year. Conrad and I talked about it, and I might have mentioned my brother-in-law's unexplained weight loss at the beginning. But neither of us said you had the big C. And I can assure you we said nothing as gruesome as you dying." There was silence on the other end. "Why? What did this guy want?"

"My business," there was an awkward laugh and more silence. "This guy says he has a business in Black Hollow. He was here on some pretext of wanting to expand his business. I guess he thought if I were dying, he could do it by buying me out."

"What did you tell the idiot?"

"I told him to get lost!" A few minutes later, A.C. ended the call. He was also aware he was losing weight and had checked with his doctor. After several tests, the doctor had confirmed the diagnosis. While his friends had made a correct assessment, A.C. was not ready to share the news. Not with anyone! And he certainly was not considering cashing in his chips. He would tell his friends. When the time was right. But this was not that time.

A.C. put an online order in a box, printed a shipping label, and set it by the door. He filled two more orders and set all three aside. They would go to the post office, but not today. Right now, he wanted to go home and forget the afternoon. He was hungry, tired, and needed *Bosch* to get his mind off things.

On his way home, A.C. picked up a hot and ready pepperoni pizza, kicked his shoes off, grabbed a brew from the fridge, and settled on the sofa. He liked *Bosch*, but tonight, he wanted something a little lighter. So he found his favorite guilty pleasure and chose *Death in Paradise*. Half the pizza was on the tray table, along with half his beer. The show was midway through the episode when his body relaxed, his eyes closed, and his breathing became slow and regular. If anyone were around, they would have heard a quiet snore from where A.C. was on the couch.

CHAPTER 7

Alan arrived Thursday at the Canario Boutique Hotel in San Juan, Puerto Rico. On Saturday, he was to meet Ross Bagdesarian at a small café on St. John Virgin Island. After checking in, he sent a brief text to Bagdesarian confirming the meeting. Alan enjoyed flying first class with all the associated perks. But getting to St. John meant a small plane from San Juan to Cyril King Airport on St. Thomas and then a water ferry to St. John.

The flight from San Juan to St. Thomas was on a small, twenty-passenger airplane. Alan's experience with these small, regional airlines was not pleasant. Not only were there no amenities, the flights were anything but a smooth ride. He dreaded these flights.

Alan downed two vodka tonics before getting into the questionable taxi to ride to the small airport. The cabs were older American models built before there was air-conditioning. The weather was sweltering, and his shirt was soaked when he reached the airport. After paying the cabbie, his stomach dropped when he turned and saw the plane—it was even smaller than he expected. It was then he wished he had opted for a third vodka-tonic. There was a small building with the word TERMINAL painted above the entrance. With trepidation, he walked through the hesitating automatic doors and handed his ticket to the attendant. He walked to the airplane and climbed a short set of stairs. He boarded and settled in for the short flight to St. Thomas.

Upon disembarking, Alan resisted the desire to kiss the ground for a safe landing. He found the taxi stand. A gray-haired man with a few missing teeth asked him, "Where ya headin' man?

"St. Thomas."

"Need to go by water taxi," Alan said, wiping the sweat from his forehead.

"Need a taxi."

"Na, man. You need Ricky." The cabbie pointed to a boy. "He'll get you there faster than a taxi. And cheaper, too.

Ricky and his rickshaw bike took him to the water taxi. Eyeing the water taxi, Alan climbed aboard with trepidation.

Two and a half hours after leaving San Juan, Alan sat across from his associate, with Lucio seated at a separate table. Alan ordered his third vodka-tonic and relaxed.

"Make it alright?" Bagdesarian asked.

"Won't know until I am back at the Canario tonight."

"Alan, you just need to relax." Bagdesarian leaned back and lowered his sunglasses to observe his guest. Bagdesarian nodded to a young islander who brought two cracked conch dishes out. Each had conch, peas, coleslaw with a side of macaroni and cheese. "They have few luxuries on this island, but the food is outstanding. They ferry it over from St. Thomas twice a day."

The islander set the meals in front of the two men and disappeared. "Relax, enjoy the view and the meal, and then we'll talk about whatever brought you down here." Bagdesarian smiled and took a bite of the conch.

A while later, the waiter removed the remnants of the meal. Bagdesarian leaned back, lit a cigar, and asked, "Well, Alan. Tell me what brought you here."

"I need a little help to seal the deal in Mexia."

"Triple M?" Bagdesarian asked.

"I believe he has cancer. It might be terminal. I need to know his doctor's name and the diagnosis. Some medical files wouldn't hurt, either," Alan explained.

"What makes you think he has cancer?"

"Overheard some of his friends talking. Could be lung cancer."

"Did you ask him about it?"

"Of course I did."

"What did he say?"

"Nothing. But there was a definite change in his body language. Can you help?"

Bagdesarian was slow to respond. Instead, he sat scrutinizing Bergman's face "It may take time," Bagdesarian said, gazing at his cigar. "I am sure I can get what you need. I need your assurances this seals the deal."

"Don't see why not," said Bergman. "If it is as bad as his friends think, he may not have all that long. You know, before being summoned to the pearly gates."

"Give me two weeks. I will let you know when the package is ready."

"Great," said Bergman. Then, pointing to Lucio, "I know he doesn't talk, but does he ever smile?"

"Same deal," Bagdesarian said, taking a drag on his cigar and blowing two smoke rings. "He smiles. People die." Bagdesarian stared at his cigar again and, without looking up, said, "Don't make him smile at you."

* * *

Alan arrived back at Black Hollow on Tuesday afternoon. The following Monday, he was in Fredericksburg at an estate sale. He picked up two lots of vinyl and CDs. He paid more than he budgeted, but still felt he would make a return on this investment.

After loading his purchases in his car, Alan checked his cell for messages. Nothing. He checked his email. More orders and nothing else.

* * *

A week later, Alan was at his storage unit, pulling things together to fulfill the orders he had received. ABM's business had seen a significant improvement and was making money. Not the money A.C. made. But he could now live off what he earned and keep his investors happy. He paused and wondered how his new pal was doing.

On returning home, Alan passed a FedEx truck as he turned down his street. He pulled to the side and watched the truck through his side mirrors. Then he watched as the truck pulled into his driveway. Excited, Alan made a U-turn and passed the truck going the other way.

There, on his front step, was a FedEx envelope. Alan picked it up and went inside. He sat down at his dining table and studied the envelope for a moment. He looked at the return address and smiled when he saw he was the sender. *Good, untraceable,* he thought. The envelope contained two things. A thumb drive that fell out as he opened it, and a bunch of papers and forms fastened by a rubber band. A yellow sticky note was on the top sheet. *This should cinch the deal.* No date or name.

Alan took the thumb drive and plugged it into a USB slot on his laptop. A few seconds later, digital copies of the papers it held appeared. In addition, there was a file with even more findings, including X-rays, lab reports, and other confidential information. Alan began going through the files. How could Bagdesarian get hold of these private documents? "Stop! Don't look a gift horse in the mouth," he said aloud.

Alan opened his last email from A.C. He typed two words. *Not Sick?* and attached a copy of the digital X-ray with the cancerous tumors circled. He deliberated for several minutes about whether he should send the email. In the end, his decision made, he hit the delete button.

Alan was many things, but he never considered himself

mean or malicious. He was unsure sending the deleted reply did not cross that line. His association with Bagdesarian and Lucio had taught him how to be stealthy in his dealings. They taught him how to set up bogus email accounts and had used these tricks when setting up his Cayman Islands operations.

Alan was about to walk away when he remembered Bagdesarian's words of warning. First, the investors were notorious for their patience and expected a sizeable return on their investment. Second, the investors were nameless and faceless. Third, they did not worry Alan. Lucio scared him, and he remembered those chilling words only too well: "Don't make him smile."

Alan retyped the email and attached the X-ray. For the subject, he typed two words, *Oh Really?* and hit send.

Bergman followed the same procedure and sent A.C. a second email. This time, the subject line had a single word: *Insurance* and the main text said: *How long before the money isn't there?* Both emails were unsigned.

*   *   *

A.C. opened his email the next day and spotted the two emails. He did not recognize the names or addresses. But then he ran an online business, and unknown names and addresses were the norm rather than the exception. He saw one with an attachment and opened it first. The digital image of his most recent check X-ray filled his seventeen-inch monitor. A yellow circle marked each suspicious spot on the image. The film his doctor shared with him had the same markings. A million questions flooded his brain, none with any answers. A.C. stared at the email with fists clenched. He read the email several times. How could his doctor be so careless? How did this confidential information get out? But A.C. both liked and trusted his doctor. The doctor had assured him that doctors don't share medical information without the patient's permission. He called the doctor to check out what was happening. The second email was even more disturbing. What money?

Mexia Police Sergeant Robert Cossotto sat across from A.C. It was Cossotto's first time in the store, and it impressed him. The officer raised the printed-out email with the X-ray and asked, "And this is your medical X-ray?"

"Yes, it is," said A.C.

"And these markings. Do you know what they mean?"

"I am very familiar with those. However, very few people know I have lung cancer. I haven't shared that information with anyone in Mexia. However, I have learned some people have openly speculated I have cancer."

"And the circles?"

A.C. took a deep breath. This was not a simple conversation. "Those represent lesions the doctor believes are cancerous."

"I'm sorry," said a contrite police sergeant.

"So am I," whispered A.C.

After a pause, the sergeant asked, "And you have talked with your doctor?"

"Yes. I was told the digitalized images were on a server outside the office. That is what I understood."

"And has your doctor's server shown signs of being hacked?"

"I don't know. My doctor was as upset as I was. He said he would call the server company and do some checking. He hasn't gotten back to me yet."

Holding up the second email, "And this other one?"

"Alan Bergman said he was aware of my cancer and offered to buy me out."

"And what did you tell him?"

I said, "Make sure the door doesn't hit you in the butt."

Cossotto took notes as they talked. Making eye contact, he asked, "Have you heard from this Bergman fellow since then?"

"No, I haven't."

"And you are sure you don't recognize these addresses?"

"Like I said. Over half the emails I get are unknown. First-time buyers and inquiries."

Both were quiet for a few minutes. Then, standing, Cossotto said, "Let me take these and show them to my chief. Maybe he has an idea how to proceed."

"Fine, I don't have a problem." A.C. gave the officer an envelope for the emails.

At the door, Cossotto turned and said. "In the meantime, follow your doctor's lead. Check your system. Run your antivirus to see if it detects spyware, malware, and similar digital intrusions."

"My tech service company will be here this afternoon. After I called them, they suggested I turn everything off. I will get a pay-as-you-go phone as a precautionary measure."

"Good idea. When you get it, let my office know your new number so we can contact you if we learn anything."

"Thank you, sergeant."

The two stood and shook hands. A.C. had posted a sign on the door announcing the store's temporary closing. He shut off the lights and retreated to his office. Exhausted, he felt as if he had just run a marathon. He thought about calling Ragsdale but remembered his friend was out of town.

It was two in the afternoon, but it felt like two in the morning. A.C. grabbed a beer, turned on Prime Video, and tried to watch a movie. He fell asleep and woke up when he heard a phone ringing. It was his old phone. He checked, and the caller's I.D. showed *unknown.* He powered down the phone, got into his Caddy, and decided he needed some ribs from Pete's.

CHAPTER 8

A.C. WAS NEVER known for his organizational skills. Wherever he went, clutter seemed to follow and become a part of his life. His office at Triple M was no exception, with boxes with orders in various stages of completion, magazines, flyers, and recent additions to his inventory. So, although his guest was also a friend, it was with some reluctance A.C. welcomed him into his office. "Sorry for the mess." He took two boxes off a chair, wiped the chair off, and offered it to his visitor.

"No problem," said Chief Musselwhite. "I've been in worse places."

The Mexia Chief of Police took the seat provided. A.C. sat across from his pal with the cluttered desk between them. While neither were avid golfers, they did enjoy spending time at the billiard hall together, however, this was an official visit, and they forwent the usual Charlie and A.C. The chief held up a clear evidence bag and asked, "When did you find this?" The bag contained a brown Bud Light bottle. It had some clear liquid in it, and someone had stuffed a multicolored rag in the bottle's mouth.

"Is it real?" asked A.C.

"Can't say for sure, but I doubt it. Especially since it was sitting on a note here in the store."

"Yeah, I guess not." A.C. couldn't take his eyes off it. "I found it when I was closing for lunch. Only had four people in the morning. Two guys in their twenties and a guy and girl who might be seniors in high school."

"Do you think one of them might be responsible?"

"I don't know. Anything is possible, I guess. I didn't recognize them."

"We'll run prints and see what turns up."

"Chief, I have not always been the quiet businessman."

"Army?"

"I cannot talk about that and other things. Forget about my first question about the bottle. We both know it isn't real. The wick was dry."

"I agree. Anything else on your mind?"

"Everyone here has been so friendly. It's just hard to wrap my head around this whole thing."

Then Musselwhite listened politely, knowing he and his friend would have to talk some more. He held up two additional evidence bags, each containing a single sheet of paper. "Cossotto showed me these. Anything else come in since you and he talked?

"Here, these came yesterday." A.C. handed him two envelopes. "I was planning to give them to Bob during lunch."

The chief took the two envelopes, opened them, and read the contents. "Somebody must be desperate for your business. Is it worth it?"

"Not if you ask me," said A.C.

"What do you think the note means? *Next time it will be real?*"

"Beats me, except I think it refers to what is in that first bag." Raising the bag with the bottle, the chief queried, "This?"

"Yes."

"Hmmm. I can't say for sure, but somebody wants you gone. And they want your business. Anyone other than Bergman making offers?"

A.C. said nothing but shook his head to show there were none.

"Any idea what is going on?" Musselwhite asked. "Look,

A.C., I want to help." He studied his friend. "I know you are not being completely honest with me." A.C. started to protest when the chief held up his hand. "Don't. I've been at this a long time. There is something there. Left over from your army days. I don't know." The chief paused again, then asked, "Anybody from your past seeking revenge?"

"No. That was years ago. And people knew me by another name back then."

"OK. Does anyone else know of your cancer?"

"The only person I told was Harold Ragsdale. He owns Cheyenne Ranch out in Erwindale in Hamilton County. However, I know others have their suspicions."

"Any chance he is behind this?"

"Not a chance."

"How can you be so sure?" asked the chief.

"Trust me, it isn't Ragsdale. Besides, he gets my business when I am gone."

"Maybe he can't wait?"

"No, you don't understand. Money is not an issue with Harry. He has more money than he knows what to do with. He paid cash for Cheyenne." A.C. took a breath and lowered his voice. "Besides, most of my stuff is already at his Cheyenne ranch. Especially the valuable stuff."

"His idea or yours?" Chief Musselwhite asked.

"Mine. Chief, you need to understand. Ragsdale and I have been to hell and back. He is the brother I never had."

"OK," said the chief.

"When the emails got more threatening and specific, I suggested we become partners. He agreed, and I moved my stock there."

"Tell me about this new partnership."

A.C. drew a deep breath and closed his eyes for a second. Then, when he opened his eyes again, he began, "Our business is not a cut-throat business. A lot of dealers have a cooperative arrangement with other dealers. For example, Ragsdale has a client needing a specific record. He knows I have it in my inventory. I may sell it to him or give it to him on consignment. Then, when he makes the sale, he pays me what he got minus an agreed-upon commission."

"This is your arrangement with Ragsdale?"

"Yes."

"So if he needs something from your stock, you give it to him?"

"On consignment."

"And he pays you when he sells the record or whatever it is?"

"In a nutshell, yes. But a part of the value of my business is my customer and

contact base. They know I am retiring, and Ragsdale is taking over the business."

"Anyone of them upset?"

"Can't imagine why," A.C. replied. "It doesn't affect them or the price of the merchandise. It is just a different name on the invoice. So, no, I can't see it being any of them."

"Well, real or fake, a Molotov cocktail is no laughing matter. My lab will try to raise any prints and analyze the liquid. I'll have more information in a few days. In the meantime, try to do business during daylight hours."

A.C. raised his eyebrows but remained silent.

"Don't take any chances. That's all I'm saying," said Musselwhite.

"I have some orders I need to finish up tonight. So, I shouldn't be too late. But for you, only during daylight hours. Promise.

"A.C., you're a good friend and well-liked in the community. A lousy pool player and you owe me a steak. I need you around to collect," Musselwhite said, with a twinkle in his eye.

"Like, you too, Charlie. Settle this weekend at Pete's."

"Oh, no. You aren't getting off that easy. You are doing the rib-eyes."

"Deal! See you Saturday night." With that, they shook

hands and A.C. walked the chief to the door. A.C. returned to his office and leaned back in his chair. He was more confused than scared. What was it about? Was Triple M worth all of this effort? What was to be gained if it burned?

* * *

The neighborhood was quiet. There were no other businesses within sight. And what few people called this neighborhood home were asleep. A brief recon came up with no doorbell-cameras. Still, he dressed in black and had a black gaiter covering the lower portion of his face.

Earlier, he had watched as Chief Musselwhite visited with his target. The chief left, but his target remained. The man knew a bell sounded when the main door opened. However, the back door was out of sight. It had nothing alerting that the door had opened.

It was just after one in the morning when he entered. He noted the propane tank for the cooker was not in its usual place. It would have been nice to have that added distraction, but he moved with confidence, knowing his plan would be effective.

A.C. was in his office. He had just finished filling the last online order, and several boxes with mailing labels were on a chair near the door. He would take them to the post office in the morning. Since his meeting with Musselwhite, his senses had been on high alert. As he locked the office, he felt the presence rather than seeing or hearing anything.

As he turned the corner to leave the store, A.C. saw a flash. He heard nothing, and his brain could not process what was happening. There was a sharp pain on the left side of his chest. Stunned, he stopped as his mind tried to assess the situation. Then his legs gave way. He fell where he was. A.C. felt, rather than heard, footsteps coming closer and strained to see his intruder. The intruder kicked him once, and he gave out a groan.

"Good. You're still with me."

Whoever it was, they needed some Listerine. The voice was a whisper. Spittle hit A.C.'s face as the man talked. His breath smelled of stale cigarette tobacco. A.C. was going into sensory overload and did not recognize the voice. Between the pain and the darkness, A.C. could not understand what was going on. Again, he sensed what was about to happen without seeing it. His eyes recorded the second flash, but his brain shut down before it could digest the information. A.C. lay still on the floor with eyes staring into the black abyss.

The intruder grabbed A.C.'s limp arms, dragged him behind the office, and grabbed a bottle from the bag he had with him. He covered the body with a foul-smelling gel. Then, using his trusty Zippo, he lit a cigarette. He took a long, satisfying drag before putting the lighter away. Next, the assailant pulled out a book of paper matches. He wedged the lit cigarette in the book of matches and with care. Bent over, he gently set them on the body. In less than five minutes, his deed was done and he left the same way he entered. He parked his car two blocks away, but the store was visible. A few minutes later, a flash lit the store's windows and the attacker heard a small explosion. If anyone were awake, they might have thought a firecracker went off, or a car backfired. Soon, the distinctive yellow-orange light of an active fire was visible, as heat shattered the glass and flames reached beyond the window.

* * *

Truck driver Bernie Williams was passing through Mexia from west to east when he noticed a strange glow south of the courthouse. He pulled his rig over and walked back to the intersection with his phone in hand. He saw the glow and what appeared to be smoke billowing from the light.

"9-1-1. What is your emergency?" the voice said on the

other end.

"My name is Bernie Williams. There appears to be a fire in a building south of the

Mexia courthouse."

"Where are you now?" the voice asked.

"I pulled my rig over so I could confirm what I saw. I am standing across from the courthouse. It appears the fire is growing." The operator kept him on the line, and within minutes, he heard the sirens and saw the flashing lights of the emergency vehicles. A police car and three fire trucks passed him, heading toward the orange glow.

*　*　*

Chief Musselwhite, Limestone County Sheriff Bart Hazelwood, and Hal Blaine, the county's newest deputy, were in Hazelwood's office with the door closed.

"The fire began overnight, and a trucker passing through called 9-1-1," began Musselwhite. "He was traveling west to east along 84 when he saw the glow south of the courthouse. He did not see any flashing lights and called it in."

"Anyone else call it in?" asked Deputy Blaine.

"Yes, about five minutes earlier, a call came in about an explosion. It appears the caller heard the explosion."

Musselwhite looked at some notes before continuing. "The fire department and Mexia Police arrived to find the building fully engulfed."

"A second alarm?" asked Hazelwood.

"No. The building is on the corner of an otherwise vacant lot. No other structures were in danger."

"How bad was it?" asked Sheriff Hazelwood, looking over his coffee.

"Bad. Really bad. From my perspective, a total loss. Talked to Fire Chief Steve Martin before coming over. He also described it as a total loss."

"What business was it?" asked Blaine.

Sheriff Hazelwood set his coffee on his desk. "Triple M."

"Triple M?" asked the deputy.

"Anthony Mottola opened a record store a few years back. He sold records, CDs, and other things. Both in the store and online. He also had a small recording studio local musicians used to record CDs. He called it *Mottola's Music and More*. To us, we referred to it as Triple M."

Hazelwood turned his attention to Chief Musselwhite. "What does A.C. have to say about the fire?"

"Haven't talked to him," said Musselwhite. "To be more specific, we can't find him. We don't know if he is out of town or—" and let the sentence die. Everyone understood the rest of the thought meant A.C. was in the building when it caught fire.

"Did we have any casualties?" asked Hazelwood.

"Chief Martin hasn't reported any. But then, we are just starting our investigation. AK47 is there now,"

"AK47?" asked Blaine.

"Our fire marshal, Anita Kerr," explained Musselwhite. "Short with fiery red hair. She barks commands in a staccato fashion. I understand she picked up the nickname at the fire academy where she was first in her class."

"What equipment is there now?" asked Blaine.

"Small truck, three firefighters, Chief Martin and AK47. Oh, and I have Bob Cossotto doing crowd control."

The sheriff stood, grabbed his Stetson, and said, "Let's head over to Triple M. Or what's left of it."

CHAPTER 9

Hal Blaine, the newest sheriff's deputy, caught the Triple M fire. He drove the sheriff to the fire scene, which took all of three minutes. Chief Musselwhite stayed at the police station. Sergeant Cossotto passed the Suburban through and followed behind. There was a fire truck on the scene. They saw three firemen inside of remnants of Mottola's Music and More. A short woman in fire department gear stood at the front of the building. Her diminutive figure filled out the gear. There was soot on her face and she held a clipboard in one hand.

"Where's Chief Musselwhite?" she asked as the two men approached.

"Short-handed, so Charlie handed us the case," the sheriff said.

"Who's the new guy?" AK asked, pointing to Blaine.

"Hal Blaine, meet our top-notch fire marshal, AK47."

"Glad to meet you." Hal gave a nod of his blue baseball cap with a sheriff's badge embroidered on it. "AK47?"

"Hal Blaine here is a former army M.P. Just out of the service and came on board last week." Turning to Blaine, Sheriff Hazelwood said, "This is Anita Kerr, our fire marshal. Don't know how, but she earned the nickname while in training. She also barks orders as if they are coming from an assault weapon. So, we let her keep her nickname."

Hal attempted a smile. AK gave him a stoic expression and a nod.

"What have we got?" asked the sheriff.

The scene was eerie and monochromatic. What movie people envision how the apocalyptic future would appear. The interior was hazy and hard on the eyes. Everything was one of a hundred fifty different shades of gray without electricity to illuminate the scene. The building still sizzled, especially when one fireman doused a hotspot. There was a pungent and acrid aroma. The metal melted, wood burned, and many of the vinyl records making up the store's contents had melted.

"Careful where you step," barked AK as they turned their Maglites on and followed her into the building.

"What's your opinion?" asked Blaine.

"Arson. No doubt."

"Why so sure?" asked Hazelwood.

AK led them to an area behind the office. One office wall was half-burned, and one wall fell towards the back, covering up whatever was underneath.

A.C. was famous for his barbecues. This was the area where he usually kept his cooker and other supplies. "Over here," said AK, pointing to a pile of rubble covered by the office wall. "Everything seems centered in this space. A minor explosion sent flames everywhere, but it all started here."

"Have you found the source of the explosion?" asked Blaine.

Before AK could answer, Sheriff Hazelwood held up his hand as he answered his phone. The conversation was one-sided and cryptic. Hazelwood lowered his hand and put his phone away. "Waco P.D. found A.C.'s car at Waco airport. They are checking the see what flight he may have taken."

"Waste of time," said Blaine. Both AK and Hazelwood looked at him. "Seen it before. Two or three times. A.C.is dead, and he is in here. Somewhere in all this mess. We just haven't found him yet. But he is in here. You can count on it.

"What makes you so sure?" asked AK.

"A couple of things. You say A.C. kept his pit and tank in here. Where is it? It did not explode, or it would have leveled the building."

"So far, you make sense. So, you think A.C. is in here?" AK asked.

"That's where I would put him," said a thoughtful Hazelwood. "The fire would destroy a lot of evidence."

"Take a whiff. What do you smell?" Both AK and Hazelwood took several whiffs of the air. "Smell the charcoal and sulphur?"

AK was the first to answer. "I noticed it a bit when I first came in. Seems a little stronger here." AK used a tool resembling a fireplace poker to lift and move rubble away from where she believed the fire began. "We have a problem." With her poker, she lifted a piece of cardboard, revealing a burned head.

As he studied the remains, Blaine said, "Told you."

"You may be right. Is this A.C.?" she wanted to know.

"Not my call," said the sheriff. "Let's call Dr. Sill and get her and her team over here."

Blaine looked at AK, giving a gesture saying, "Dr. Sill?"

"Dr. Sill is our medical examiner. The fire is out. I've determined it is arson, and we have a corpse. That's all I need. This is now the M.E.'s case."

* * *

Ten minutes later, a bright blue Tesla Falcon pulled up. The gull-wing doors opened, and a tall brunette got out. Dressed in green surgical scrubs showing off tattoos on both arms, she put on booties and a hairnet and grabbed her Maglite.

"Where's the body?" Her voice was firm and matter of fact.

"Over here." AK led her to where they had found the body.

A gray Ford Explorer pulled up. The driver began unloading lights and a generator. He put on booties, a cap covering his hair, and a net covering his beard. Then, with a light in each hand, he started toward the door and stopped.

"Can I bother one of you to lead the way?"

Blaine turned his Maglite on and led the new man to the

crime scene. The assistant and Sill talked for a few minutes, and he returned to his vehicle and brought back a third lamp. He attached extension cords to the generator in front of the store. The generator came to life, and the interior of the building lit up with a bright white light.

Sill came out, got a sketch pad from the trunk of her car, and went back in. The assistant came out and grabbed a camera from the back seat of his truck. Flashes from the camera's strobe light appeared as flashes of lightning. Sill's assistant took pictures while Sill was busy sketching the scene on her scratch pad.

"Sheriff, we have exposed the body," said Sill. Blaine and Hazelwood made their way back to the lights.

"Cause of death?" asked Hazelwood.

"Not the fire, that's for sure."

AK joined them and asked, "How can you be so sure?"

"Two holes in the body that weren't put there by God. One to the chest just above the heart, and one between the eyes." She watched the reactions of the others.

"Anything else?" asked AK.

"Body is your point of origin for the fire."

"Spontaneous combustion?" asked Blaine and smiled.

"I have read reports of spontaneous combustion, and I can assure you, deputy, this body did not spontaneously burst into flame. Instead, this unsub doused the body with a combustible compound. At this point, I can't say with any certainty what that was, except it wasn't gasoline."

AK spoke up. "There are reports of arsonists using a new gelatin compound. The arsonist smears it on a surface, and then heats the surface. Not ignited as you would gasoline. Instead, they place a source of heat on the covered area. When the gel reaches a critical temperature, it ignites. There are reports minor explosions in connection with this method. This sends the flaming substance over a wide area."

"Charlie said something about someone reporting an explosion about the time the trucker reported the fire," said

Sheriff Hazelwood. Then looking down at the body, "Is it A.C.?"

"Hard to tell. The body is that of a big man. It is possible, even probable, but I cannot confirm without an autopsy. Has anybody seen Mr. Mottola since the fire?"

"No. Waco P.D. found A.C.'s car at Waco airport," explained the sheriff.

Sill was kneeling next to the body, then stood to face the others. "The body is burned and contorted, but I believe I can extract enough DNA for comparison. Can you get me some of Mr. Mottola's DNA for comparison?"

"We can go by his house to see what we can find," said Blaine.

"No," replied Hazelwood. "We may not need a warrant, but I want to get one just in case."

"Just in case?"

"Just in case that body is someone else, and A.C. caught a flight out of Waco," said the sheriff. "Call Judge Linda Albert. She is at home and should sign the paper. This body is not going to get up and walk out of here. So we have time."

"I've called for the wagon," said Sill. "It will be another two hours at least before we can get him out of there. There is the body's condition, but it is a mess here. We don't want anyone getting hurt."

Hazelwood's phone buzzed. He looked at the caller, pushed the green phone button, and listened. "OK, thanks," he said. "Blaine is right. A.C. did not board a flight out of Waco. Waco CSI is on the scene now and processing the car."

"Let's go," the sheriff said to his deputy. "There is nothing left for us to do here. When we have confirmation from Sill, then we can move." The two made their way out of the building and drove back to the office.

CHAPTER 10

Blaine walked Musselwhite to the Sheriff's Office conference room. Sheriff Hazelwood arrived a few minutes later and offered water and coffee. He took a seat at the table. Lead investigator Blaine sat at the head of the table with Hazelwood and Musselwhite.

"Thank you for coming in," said the sheriff. "I'm sorry for your loss. I am aware you and A.C. were friends."

"Thanks," said Musselwhite. After a brief pause, he said, "So, someone shot him before burning the building?"

"Appears so. Any idea why?"

"What about the fire?"

"The autopsy indicated there was no smoke in the lungs. He was dead when the fire started."

"And—" Musselwhite let the sentence die.

"Charlie," began Blaine, "Looks like the chest bullet came first, followed by the headshot. According to Sill, the shooter wanted Mottola to see what was coming."

"So," the chief said, "a pro?"

"Hard to imagine an amateur being that meticulous."

"Are you saying it was a hit?"

"Well—" began Blaine when the sheriff cut him off.

"Charlie. Do you know why someone would hit your friend? Did he say anything about his past or—?"

"No. I understand he was both an army brat and served as well. He wouldn't talk about the period between the army and his arrival here."

"He was your friend, right?" asked Blaine.

"I didn't know him long, but I considered him a friend." Then, being quiet and looking down, Musselwhite's face grew a wry smile. "I am going to miss that old pool shark," he said.

"Pool shark?" asked Blaine.

"Yeah. Neither of us had a poker face. Our tells were never subtle, so we skipped any type of card game. But A.C. was a genius around a pool table and played a mean game of bank pool. I could hold my own when we played numbered pool."

"Numbered pool?"

"You don't play billiards, do you, son?"

Blaine's hair bristled at the being called *son*, but kept his cool and said he hadn't.

"Well, numbered pool is where a select number of balls are used. The most popular game is eight-ball. However, you can start with three balls and work your way up from there. His real expertise was bank pool. You score a point by putting a ball in a pocket after banking your cue ball off the side of the table. I never came close to challenging him."

After a brief pause, Hazelwood said, "Not to change the topic, but you said you had something for us?"

"Yes." Musselwhite laid down two folders and an evidence bag containing an empty bottle. Then, ignoring his items, he said, "You should know A.C. had cancer."

"What kind? How bad?"

"He never talked about his health or what he did after the army before he got here. Then, one night while we were playing eight-all, he said he was pooped and let it slip. He said his cancer was getting the best of him. I pressed, but he would not talk about it anymore. I noticed some weight loss and even joked I could use his diet to lose a few pounds. He said you don't want this diet."

"What was your take?" asked Hazelwood.

"Just guessing, I would say the cancer was advanced. When

I pressed, he got upset and said, "Charlie. Just drop it! OK?" and I did.

"OK, advanced." Blaine made some notes on a legal pad. "Anything else?"

"I got the impression it was terminal."

Watching Musselwhite for clues, he said, "Days, weeks, months, years?"

"Can't say," said Musselwhite. "A.C. was a private person. As far as I know, he only mentioned the cancer to two people. He let it slip with me, but he may have told Ragsdale more. I got the impression he and Ragsdale had history. A diagnosis of cancer is not something you always want to keep to yourself. It has been my experience, they tell someone. Family-or a close friend."

"You were his friend," Hazelwood said.

"Yes, but we were not close. Not like Ragsdale. I know A.C. would go to Ragsdale's ranch, and Ragsdale would visit him in town."

"You said a person might tell their family. Did Mottola have a family?" asked Blaine.

"He had a daughter. I believe they were not close, and he lost track of her. At some point, he said something about A&M. That could be why he settled here in Mexia. A.C. said staying in Texas would make it easier for him to find her."

"So, you have no way to get a hold of her?"

"A.C. told me he and his wife separated for a while and later divorced. His ex-wife died three or four years ago. Don't think he ever said how. A.C. believed his daughter dropped Mottola for her mother's maiden name, Sager, as her last name. Carol was her given name."

"How hard did he try to find her?" asked Hazelwood.

"I can't say. A.C. said he hated FERPA since it kept getting in the way. Privacy and all that, you know. Plus, he could not establish he was her father. He even talked of a P.I. I can't say for sure he hired one."

Hazelwood looked at Blaine and said, "FERPA will not be a problem for us."

After a lull in the conversation, Blaine asked, "What is that?" pointing to the folders.

"Can't say for sure. Could be a suspect. Or maybe only a person of interest," said Musselwhite.

"Does this person have a name?" asked Blaine.

"Alan Bergman. A.C. told me this Alan Bergman fellow has stopped by his business a few times. Seems Bergman has a similar business in Black Hollow. He said he was aware of A.C.'s cancer and offered to buy Triple M."

"What did A.C. say?" asked Hazelwood.

"My understanding is, he told Bergman to bug off. But I also think it bothered him."

Hazelwood asked, "What makes you say that?"

"According to what A.C. told me, that is when he started moving his inventory out of the store and moved it to Ragsdale's Cheyenne Ranch."

The chief opened the first folder and handed Blaine and Hazelwood copies of the folder's contents. "For about a month, A.C. was targeted by cyber harassment. It started out with these emails."

"A.C. give you these?" Blaine asked.

"Why?" Hazelwood followed up with.

"I think he was worried. Maybe not so worried as suspicious. He told me it was not the emails, but who they came from that bothered him." Blaine pointed out they were unsigned. "A.C. said he believed Bergman was behind them but could not prove it. A.C. said there was something off about the guy and that set off all sorts of alarms in his brain. I believe A.C. called us to have a paper trail should something happen to him."

"OK. Alan Bergman."

"They started out just as annoying and unwanted," Musselwhite said.

Blaine read the emails, then looked at the chief. "Anything

else?"

Musselwhite took the folder back, opened the second folder, and handed them copies of the contents. "The first is a print of a chest X-ray showing the tumors. This is confidential information. As far as A.C. knew, only his doctor had copies of his X-rays."

"And the other?" asked the sheriff.

"Quotes from his medical record where the doctor interpreted the X-ray and diagnosed cancer."

"Did the doctor have the only copies?" asked Blaine.

"Yes. Cossotto had A.C. call his doctor on speakerphone. Cossotto explained the situation and with the doctor's permission and he used a hand-held digital recorder to record the call." Musselwhite pulled out a cassette and handed it to Blaine. "That's the conversation."

Blaine asked, "I'll listen later, but what did the doctor say?".

"The doctor was stunned and could not explain how anyone could have gotten their hands on the X-rays or his notes. He assured A.C. his office did not release the information but would investigate."

Blaine set the cassette on the table. "What about that bottle?"

"A.C. found the bottle in his store after he closed for lunch. He recognized it to be a Molotov cocktail. There was a clear liquid inside and a warning written on the bottle."

Blaine picked up the bottle and the note. "*Next time it will be real.*"

"A.C. was smart enough to leave it in place and called me. So I bagged it and sent it to the lab."

"The liquid?" asked the sheriff.

"Water." The chief handed the report to Blaine. "Distilled water."

"Prints?"

"Wiped clean."

"Any idea who did it?" asked Hazelwood.

"Nope. Someone placed it on a stack of vinyl records just

out of sight of the camera."

"That all?"

"No, there were hate mails and threatening phone calls and graffiti."

"When did you get all this?" asked Blaine.

"Less than a week before the fire."

"You think Bergman is behind this?"

"He is number one on my list."

"Why? Why not Ragsdale?" chimed in Hazelwood.

"Motive. Bergman wanted Triple M and used some clandestine tactics," said Musselwhite.

"The emails and fake Molotov cocktail," Hazelwood repeated.

"That is my conclusion."

"And Ragsdale?" asked Blaine.

"No motive. A.C. said most of his merchandise is already in Ragsdale's hands. And there may be a business deal giving Ragsdale access to everything."

Blaine checked his notes, picked up the emails, bottle, and forensics report, then excused himself.

Musselwhite watched Blaine leave. "He's a good cop."

"Deputy," corrected Hazelwood.

"Whatever. I'm just glad I am on his side."

CHAPTER 11

SHERIFF HAZELWOOD SLUMPED in the visitor's chair while Blaine hunched over his desk, re-examining his notes. "Well, did you get anywhere with what Charlie brought over?"

"Not really," said Blaine. "Whoever wrote these emails was very good. They hid their tracks very well. But Bart, whoever wrote these emails, did not want to be found. The account name is bogus, and the IP address is bogus. Our techies could not trace where these originated."

"Not surprising, the computer was chicken-fried," said Hazelwood.

"Yeah, but there were emails from the same address on his personal computer. In most cases, they can backtrack to a specific computer. This guy, though. He knew what he was doing. I doubt this is the first time he's gone stealth."

Both were silent as the street noise permeated the room. "Something's not right. We must be missing a key point, but I can't put my finger on it." Hazelwood stood and looked out the window. Again, the street noise permeated the room when Hazelwood abruptly turned. Then to no one, he asked, "Why would a guy wanting to buy a business shoot and kill the seller?"

"And then torch the business?" Hazelwood added. "It doesn't make any sense."

"That has been bothering me as well," said Blaine. "It makes little sense. Maybe we can get some answers when we get this Bergman fella in here."

"What if it isn't him?"

"He may not have committed murder and arson, but he knows who did. He may not have done the deed, but he is involved. And that, my friend, you can take to the bank!" The two stood looking at each other. In a softer tone, Hazelwood asked, "Any luck in finding him?"

"Not so far. The house is empty, and his car is gone. There was no mail in his mailbox. We checked with neighbors, and they said he packed up his car early one morning last week. Thursday or Friday. We checked with the post office and there is a hold on his mail until Monday. We'll make another run out to his place on Tuesday."

"Any idea where he is?" asked Hazelwood.

"With his mail on hold, we are pretty sure it was voluntary. The old guy across the street said he was a hunter. They had shared hunting stories while waiting at Cabela's a few weeks ago. It's possible he went hunting. If he did, then he may not be our guy."

The sheriff studied his desk, resting his weight on his knuckles. Hazelwood almost whispered, "Yeah, but that doesn't mean he didn't order the hit."

"Goes back to motive," Blaine said.

"I agree."

"It makes no sense burning down the business you were trying to buy."

Hazelwood raised his head. "What about the daughter? Any progress?"

"Musselwhite has located her and talked to her on the phone."

"Where'd they find her?"

"Montgomery, where she runs a large animal vet clinic with a friend."

"I understand he and Mitch Miller will drive to Montgomery to talk with her tomorrow."

"Know her father is dead?"

"I believe they told her."

"Reaction?"

"Pretty much what you'd expect. Combination of shock and disbelief."

"Why aren't you going?"

"Overkill. Besides, Charlie and Mitch were friends with her dad. That could help her take it all in. So I'll get my turn when she comes in."

"And Ragsdale?" asked the sheriff.

"Ragsdale will be here on Wednesday. He was at a record show. He has the *Trib.* on his phone, and that's how he learned about the fire. So he called Charlie, and they scheduled an appointment for Wednesday."

"What time?"

"We'll meet in Charlie's office—that was Charlie's suggestion. He asked me after they set the meeting up. I saw no problem. You?"

"No. Let's keep everyone comfortable. For now, anyway. Ragsdale have an alibi?"

"Guess we will find out on Wednesday."

* * *

Bergman wore casual khakis, an Izod polo shirt, and deck shoes when he welcomed Blaine into his home office. Unlike A.C.'s office, Bergman's was neat, clean, and well organized.

Blaine began the conversation. "I understand you were interested in buying out Mr. Mottola. How did you learn it was for sale?"

Bergman ignored the question. "I approached him with an offer?"

"Why? Did Mr. Mottola suggest his business was for sale?" asked Blaine.

"No. It's just something I heard."

"Where did you hear it?"

"Wait," said Bergman, holding up a hand. "Am I a suspect? You think I had something to do with his death?"

"Did you?"

"I won't even honor that with a response. Look. I am a businessman and I learned one of my competitors might be inclined to sell. I made an offer. That's all!"

"Is it?"

"I liked A.C., and what happened to him… Well, he did not deserve it. But remember, I wasn't in town when all this happened."

"I'm sorry, but this is a murder investigation. We are talking to everyone who had dealings with Mr. Mottola in the past few weeks."

"Murder? I thought he died when his business burned."

Blaine showed no reaction. "Mr. Bergman. Someone shot Mr. Mottola. Twice. And then torched the building to cover up the murder."

"I don't know anything about any fire, let alone a shooting." Bergman's tone became more defensive.

"I didn't say you did," said Blaine. "I am just trying to find out how you came to make an offer to buy a business. A business that was not for sale."

"Like I said, someone said A.C. may be in the market to unload. So I made him an offer. End of story."

"Did he accept the offer?" Blaine asked.

"No."

"You said you learned he may be in the market to unload Triple M."

"Yes," said Bergman. "Listen, should I get an attorney?"

"Do you need an attorney?"

"I don't know. What do you think?"

"Not for me to say."

"I am thinking I should have an attorney."

Blainelooked up from taking notes and said, "Of course, that is your prerogative. You still haven't answered my question."

"Am I a suspect in A.C.'s death?"

"No, you are not a suspect. We are talking to those who had dealings with Mr. Mottola. We are focusing our attention on the weeks before his death." Blaine watched for a reaction and got none. "You have been out of town. Do you mind telling me where you've been?"

"Montana," Bergman said.

"What drew you to Montana?"

"Deer. It's hunting season up there, and a friend invited me up for a week."

"Anyone there able to confirm you were there?"

"Of course," said Bergman. "I stayed with Martin Robbins." Bergman took a sticky note and wrote down Robbins' phone number. "Here is his number. You can call him, and he will verify I was there." Bergman picked up his phone and opened the photo gallery. "Here are pictures. This is us with an elk he shot. Is that good enough for you?"

Blaine glanced at the pictures, then said, "You never said how you discovered Mr. Mottola might want to sell his business."

"I didn't?"

"No," Blaine said in a monotone voice. "You did not."

"Look, sheriff."

"Deputy. I am a sheriff's deputy, not a sheriff," Blaine corrected.

"You came in here and suggested I may be involved in A.C.'s death in what I would call an accusatory tone."

"You always called him A.C.?"

Exasperated, Bergman let out a breath. "Yes. That is what A.C. said his friends called him."

"Were you friends?"

"I think this conversation is over. I think it's time you left," said Bergman.

"You still haven't answered my question." Blaine did not move.

"Like A.C., I attend music conventions and estate sales. So

someone must have said something. You know, at one of those things. To tell the truth, I can't remember."

Bergman walked Blaine to the door. They did not shake hands. Blaine handed Bergman a business card and said, "Call me if you remember where you learned Mr. Mottola might want to sell."

"I will, deputy." Bergman stood at the door and watched the deputy drive away. Once the car was out of sight, Bergman opened his phone and pushed a button. When a voice answered, Bergman asked, "What have you done?"

CHAPTER 12

Harold Ragsdale sat on a bench in the Mexia Police Department foyer while waiting for Chief Musselwhite to arrive. The chief greeted his visitor and escorted him back to the conference room. Ragsdale was tall, dressed in a Western shirt, jeans, snakeskin boots, and a gray Stetson. "Need anything? Water? Coffee? Excuse me for a minute. I need to make a quick call. I'll be right back."

Ragsdale accepted a bottle of water and admired the pictures on the conference room wall. They were of Mexia and the surrounding areas. Some dated back to when they founded the town in the 1870s.

Musselwhite returned to the room and stood next to Ragsdale. They both looked at a picture of an old post office. "1872," said Musselwhite. "That's when we got our first post office. The founding fathers incorporated the city the following year."

"I didn't realize Mexia had such a history."

"Most people are in the same boat." The chief walked to the conference table. "Have a seat." They sat across from each other. "I just called Deputy Blaine, the lead detective on this case. He's on his way over now."

"Deputy?" said Ragsdale with a raised eyebrow.

"We are short-handed, and I asked Sheriff Bart Hazelwood to handle the investigation. Hal Blaine is the deputy in charge. He's new, but has worked a few murder cases for the army."

The chief was giving more background on the case when Blaine walked in.

Musselwhite made the introductions. Blaine and Ragsdale shook hands and sat down. Blaine sat across from Ragsdale, next to the chief. "Thank you for coming in. I understand you are just back from a convention?"

* * *

"Vegas. They have a big music festival every even year. In fact, that's how Anthony and I got reacquainted. We did some government work together. But that was in a different lifetime."

"Ever call him A.C.?"

"He hated the whole Anthony thing. He said it sounded so formal and pompous and had everyone call him A.C. As far as I am aware, I am the only person he allowed to call him Anthony." Ragsdale had a smile on his face, recalling this memory. "I cannot wrap my head around the fact he died. And such a violent death at that. But the Anthony I knew wouldn't hurt a soul."

"Were you close?" asked Blaine.

"At one time we were but then we lost touch with one another. We used to run in the same circles. Sometimes, we would get together and swap war stories when we were at the same festival. But that was then. Today? I have to say no, we were not close. At least, not until I moved to Texas."

"Why did you move to Texas?" asked Musselwhite.

"Money. It's all about the money. In California, I gave more and more of my money to the government. So when I heard Anthony moved here, I called him, and he convinced me Texas was good for business. The state would let me keep more of my money."

"You were competitors, then?" asked Blaine.

"Yes, and no. We both dealt in the same genre of entertainment collectibles. A.C. was more big-city stuff from

New York and Hollywood. I was more country. So much of my stuff came out of the middle of the country."

"Nashville?"

"Yes, I had a lot of stuff from Nashville. But also Louisiana, Philly, and Detroit. Where a lot of headliners got their start."

"The word on the street," said Blaine. "A.C. helped you buy your ranch out in Erwindale."

"Cheyenne Ranch. Yes, he put me in touch with a broker in Hamilton."

"I understand you paid cash," said Musselwhite. He liked Ragsdale, but he was also skeptical.

"I've been lucky with some of my investments over the years. Money has never been a problem. Besides, I recouped more than I spent selling my property in California. I sold my house and the rental houses I owned."

"Did you have a business arrangement with A.C.?" asked Blaine.

"Not at first. Then two things happened."

"Two things?" asked Musselwhite.

"The big C raised its ugly head. Anthony told me it numbered his days, and he wanted to fade away from the business. However, it was not his style to throw the proverbial towel in and quit. He enjoyed doing things on his terms."

"And the second?"

"Alan Bergman," said Ragsdale.

"So, you know Mr. Bergman?"

"Know of him. Don't know him. However, I have never had the pleasure of meeting the idiot!"

"What can you tell me about him?"

"Only what Anthony shared. Bergman got this notion Anthony was sick and dying."

"He *was* sick and dying, right?"

"True. But it was not common knowledge. I think he might have let it slip with

you," and nodded to the chief. "However, if I am not

mistaken, I am the only one with whom he shared the ugly truth. Anyway, he might want to sell Triple M. I guess Bergman dismissed Anthony's denial of his illness. At some point, Bergman said he had proof of the illness and its seriousness."

"Are you and A.C. in business together?"

Ragsdale took a deep breath, then said, "It's complicated. It is true, we have a business arrangement. However, we are not partners in the legal sense. We considered ourselves partners but we don't have the legal documents."

"Enlighten me," said Blaine.

"There are a ton of people doing the same thing Anthony and I do. Not only here in the States, but globally. It is not uncommon for one dealer to work with another. Anthony and I developed an informal alliance. So, if a client of mine wants a specific item that another dealer has—"

"Like, A.C.?"

"Yes." Ragsdale confirmed, "the dealer would give me the item, and I would sell it for an agreed-upon price. Then, after the sale, I give the dealer the money, less a twenty percent commission."

"Is that your arrangement with A.C.?"

"A little more formal, but yes."

"What do you mean, a little more formal?"

Ragsdale leaned forward with his arms on his knees. "You need to understand Anthony was sick. He was aware he was dying, and the doctors gave him less than a year. Then this Bergman fellow shows up with his high-pressure tactics. The emails, letters, and other intimidating factors."

"So, you were aware of the emails?" This was more of a statement than a question.

"Yes," said Ragsdale. "I encouraged him to go to the police. But he first wanted to safeguard his investment. That's why we moved all but the junk out to Cheyenne. We have them stored in a spare bungalow."

"And the formal part?"

"Anthony's attorney, Mitch Miller, drew up a contract. I get ten percent of everything he sells as payment for storing the inventory."

"Ever have any arguments? Ever want him hurt?" asked Musselwhite.

"What? No! Never! I told you we had a relationship in another life. We were brothers from a different mother and I could never harm a hair." He stopped, trying to stifle a laugh.

"Go on," prodded Blaine.

"I was going to say a hair on his head, but he took care of that. Anyway, there is no way I could ever hurt him. So, two or three times a month, I would drive over to Mexia. We would spend some time on the lake. Or he'd come to Cheyenne. We would ride a little, sit around the fire pit, and tell stories."

* * *

"What can you tell me about his daughter?" asked Blaine.

"Only that her name is Carol. I understood she dropped Anthony's last name in favor of her mother's maiden name, Sager."

"Any idea where she is?"

"No. But I am confident Anthony wanted to find her."

"Was he having any luck?" asked Blaine.

"He told me he went online and found a picture from an A&M yearbook."

"Anything else?"

"No. Anthony was talking to a P.I., but I don't think he followed through. Following his divorce, he gave up all parental rights. I think they were living in or around Nashville then. But that is only a guess."

Blaine reviewed his notes and announced, "I think we have everything we need for the moment. Thank you for coming in, Mr. Ragsdale."

"One more thing," said Ragsdale without getting up. "I

assume you are trying to locate the daughter."

"We are," said Blaine.

"Well, if you find her, please give me a call. As you know, Anthony came into a windfall with the real-estate ventures. He put that windfall in a trust. For her."

"How much money?" asked Musselwhite.

"My guess is six figures, but I can't say for sure." Then Ragsdale stood and shook hands. "I'd like to tell her about my friend. She needs to know the friend we called A.C."

"Amen to that," said Musselwhite. "We'll keep you posted."

Musselwhite called for an officer to escort Ragsdale to the foyer. "He's hiding something."

"Yes, he is," said Blaine.

"Do you believe him?"

"I believe he was truthful about what he said. However, I am not convinced he has told us everything."

"Do you think he is involved?"

"What? In the murder?" asked Blaine. The chief nodded. "No. There is a softness in his voice when he talks about A.C. I heard him say they were friends. A.C. called him the brother he never had."

"So, what is bothering you?"

"There is more to this story. He is not being completely honest. However, unless what he is hiding turns out to be related to this case, I don't see the need to push any harder."

CHAPTER 13

A SHORT WOMAN with short, dark curly hair approached the window in the law office of Mitch Miller. "Hello. My name is Carol Sager. I believe Mr. Miller is expecting me." The tone was soft. Her voice revealed her nervousness. Carol was not sure why she agreed to the meeting. She understood it was about her father, a man hadn't seen in a quarter century. Bitter after her father abandoned the family, she cut all ties to him. She changed her name from Carol Mottola to Carol Sager. Sager was her mother's maiden name.

"Ah, Miss Sager?" Mitch said as he walked over to her. Miller gave a warm smile when he saw her, and his voice was friendly. For Carol, this was not a friendly meeting and she remained aloof. They did a perfunctory handshake, and she followed him back to his office. It startled Carol to see a deputy sheriff waiting for them in the office.

"Miss Sager, this is Deputy Hal Blaine, one of our deputy sheriffs. He is the lead investigator on your father's case." Blaine stood as Mitch motioned everyone to sit around the table in his office.

Blaine nodded to Carol and said, "I am sorry for your loss."

Carol sat down, folded her hands in her lap and in a soft voice thanked the deputy for his condolences.

"Miss Sager, I am aware you have not had recent contact with your father."

"He abandoned my mother and me twenty-five years ago,"

she said, hiding any emotion.

"What can you tell me about your father or his family?"

"Nothing."

"What did your mother tell you about your father?"

"Not much. He was not a welcome topic of conversation in the house."

"What did she tell you about their divorce?"

"Like I said, he was not a welcome topic of conversation. We did not talk about him."

"Did she say why he left?"

"No. Where are you going with this?"

Blaine leaned on the table and clasped his hands. "Miss Sager. Someone murdered your father. They shot him twice and then burned his business to hinder the discovery of his murder. You father had not lived in Mexia for very long and our information on him is sketchy. I am sorry for these questions. I am sure they must be difficult for you." He paused and watched Carol. "I only have a few more questions. Are you alright? Or do we need to take a break?"

"I'm sorry. I'm OK. Mom never talked about him, their marriage, or the divorce. It seems like he never existed. Except for two things."

Blaine's attention perked up. "Two things?"

"When Mom died, I found two pictures in a nightstand drawer. One was of her wedding day. She was beautiful and looked happy."

"And the second?"

"Mom, with a man in uniform. An army uniform. My father, I guess. Anyway, he looked like the man in the wedding picture."

"You did not see them before?"

"No. She never had them out."

"What can you tell me about your grandmother? You father's mother?"

"Nothing. I don't remember ever meeting her."

"Your grandmother was a long-time resident of Mexia."

"I had a grandmother in Mexia?" she said, startled by the revelation.

Blaine paused before continuing. "Your grandmother passed away a few years ago. Your father was an only child, and he inherited a lot of property. He sold most of it. However, he had a store just south of town."

"After you called, I read about the fire. Is that the building that burned?"

"Yes. About a month ago. We found your father inside the building. They had shot him. Twice."

There was a gasp. This was the first time Carol showed any emotion. "Where is he? I mean, where is he buried?"

"Your father was a veteran, and as per his instructions, we cremated him. He is at the Veteran Cemetery outside of Killeen."

Miller watched Carol and said, "If you would like, I would be happy to drive you."

"No," she said, cutting him off. "Maybe someday, but not right now."

"I am unaware of your family's history or what kind of father he was to you or a husband to your mother back then."

"My father was not a nice man." Carol focused on the deputy. "He abandoned us when I was a baby. I have had no contact with him."

Blaine let Carol vent, then said, "He adopted his initials as his name, A.C. He was soft-spoken and kind-hearted. A.C. was well-liked."

"If he was so well-liked, why was he murdered?" Her voice wavered in confusion.

"As Mr. Miller told you, I am investigating his murder. I am trying to learn as much as I can about him to bring his killer to justice.

"I am not sure how I can help. As I said, my father was not a nice man. I was a baby when he left. Mom never talked about him. One time when I was a teenager, I pressed her for more information. All she said was he drank too much. So, when I turned eighteen, I went to court and changed my name. Mom never had a picture of him in the house. It was not until she was gone that I found the two pictures. The ones I told you about. Mom said the divorce forced him to give up all parental rights. I guess that is why I never heard from him."

"So, any idea who or why someone would want to hurt him?"

"Sure. I grew up missing my father and hating him. I had dreams of a loving relationship and then images of a drunk father. Well, you get the idea." Her emotions surfaced, and she wiped a tear from her eye for the first time. "But I cannot help you in finding anyone who would want to shoot and burn his body. I can't imagine anyone would want to do that to another human being."

"You are a veterinarian?" Miller said to ease tensions.

"Yes. I work at a large-animal clinic outside Montgomery."

"How's it going?" asked Miller.

"It's going. I'm not getting rich, but I'm doing alright."

"Are you married? Kids?"

"No. I am engaged to Philip Collins. Philip is a lawyer in Montgomery."

"Great. Have you set a date yet?"

"No, not yet. His family is from North Star, Ohio. They are farmers. We are going up in a few weeks so I can meet them." She had a pleasant smile when she talked about her future. "Looks like we may need to postpone that with my father's murder and all."

"There is no reason to postpone your trip," Blaine assured her. "The investigation is tedious. But, given you were not involved in your father's life, I see no reason to alter your plans."

Miller waited to see if Blaine was going to say anything else, then asked, "Can you stay in town for another day? There is someone I want you to meet."

"I did not plan on staying, so I didn't bring any extra clothes with me. And I have my practice."

"No problem," said Miller.

"Who do you want me to meet?" asked Carol.

"I have two people who want to meet you. Police Chief Musselwhite and Harold Ragsdale. They were friends of your father's and have expressed a desire to meet you. Mr. Ragsdale has some business to discuss with you."

"Business? What kind of business?" asked a startled Carol.

"Ragsdale was your father's friend and business partner. As his sole heir, there are some things he needs to discuss with you," said Miller. "I believe your father also left you some money as well. Mr. Ragsdale is the executor of his will and is the caretaker of the funds."

"I never knew my father, and I know nothing about his business. He can have it all," said Carol.

Making physical contact for the first time, Miller said, "Carol, we have thrown a lot at you in a brief time. I cannot imagine the mixed feelings you must be experiencing. Your meeting with the chief and Mr. Ragsdale is important. But that meeting does not need to happen now. I know what they have to say, and I think you should hear them out."

"If you know what they want to say, why don't you just say it now?"

"It's not my story to tell." Everyone sat without speaking.

"OK," Carol said. "Let me get back to my clinic and check my schedule. Then I will call you and see what I can work out."

"Miss Sager," Blaine said, "that will be fine. But there is nothing so urgent you must rearrange your plans. Just let Mr. Miller know when he can set up the meet."

"And the business deal?"

Miller said, "Take your time. When you are ready, we will take care of it."

Blaine took her contact information and thanked her for coming. Miller walked to the door and watched her pull out of the parking lot.

"Well, what do you think?" asked Miller when he returned.

Everyone was standing looking out the window. Musselwhite said, "Well, I would never have picked A.C. as a drunk."

Almost as a whisper, Blaine said, "Everyone has their secrets," then turned and left the room.

CHAPTER 14

JIMMY BUFFET WAS on stage when Alan saw Bagdesarian at a booth in the corner. Lucio was at a nearby table, with an eye on the room. Bagdesarian raised a hand, signaling Alan to join them. Alan nodded his head, and headed that way. After Alan sat down, he was aware Lucio moved to a point where he could keep both men in his eyesight.

"So, what has got you so hot and bothered?" asked Bagdesarian. "Your tone on our last call was none too friendly."

"What in the blazes did you do?" demanded a red-faced Alan. Veins were visible in his neck.

"Back it up, my friend."

Lucio pointed a finger gun in Alan's direction and, with a smile on his face, pulled the trigger. Alan became quiet.

"Have a drink." Bagdesarian motioned a waitress over and ordered a margarita for his guest. "We are in a public place. The last thing either of us wants is to make a scene. So, sit back, listen to Jimmy. Alan, you need to learn how to relax!"

"But—"

"No buts. You need to calm down or it will end with you and Lucio there," nodding in Lucio's direction, "having a very short conversation. It will end with you forever regretting walking through that door," pointing toward the front door. "Capisce?"

With some hesitation, Alan took a sip of his margarita and tried to relax. He tried to lean back, but his tense muscles made the position uncomfortable. Especially with Lucio staring him down and occasionally allowing a smile to be seen. Jimmy finished his signature song, *Margaritaville,* and left the stage.

Alan downed what remained of his drink. Observing Lucio out of the corner of his eye, he asked Bagdesarian, "Now, can we talk?"

With a raised hand, Bagdesarian said, "Just a minute." He motioned Lucio to the table, and the two had a quiet conversation. Lucio stood, glanced at Bergman, then nodded to his boss and left.

"Where's he going?" Alan asked as he eyed Lucio heading out the door.

"Don't worry about him. Tell me, Alan, what has you so upset?"

"A.C."

Bagdesarian raised his eyebrows and asked, "The record store owner?"

"Yes. His building burned to the ground."

"Anyone hurt?"

"You know there was. They found A.C. in the ashes of his building."

"Burned to death? Terrible, terrible, terrible. Not a pleasant way to go," Bagdesarian said with a look of caution directed at Bergman.

"You know very well he did not burn to death. You shot him. Twice!" Alan could feel the heat rising to his throbbing head..

"I did, did I? Maybe. I am beginning to suspect you did it." Bagdesarian smirked fractionally.

"Hogwash!" Alan said. His elevated blood pressure made it difficult to focus.

"There you go again," Bagdesarian said. "You need to calm down and control yourself. I want to help, but you cannot, and will not, create a scene. Not here. Not now. Capisce?"

Alan looked away, said nothing. He took a deep breath and held it. As he exhaled, he nodded understanding.

"I am sorry your friend is dead. I still don't get why you are so upset. You said you didn't do it, so what is the problem?"

"I know *you* did it!"

"What?" asked Bagdesarian in surprise.

"We both know you either did it or you had it done. I just don't understand why?"

"Whoa, there, pardner." In a slow and deliberate tone, Bagdesarian said just above a whisper, "Be careful what you say. Especially when accusing people of murder."

"They murdered your grandfather in the seventies."

"Early eighties," Bagdesarian corrected, "What does that have to do with your friend?"

"They shot your grandfather twice," Bergman said, getting his emotions under control.

"Yes. One in the chest. And one in the head. So, what?"

"Well, they shot A.C. twice."

"Let me guess. Once in the chest and a second in the head?" asked Bagdesarian.

"Yes."

"And you think it was me?"

"Yes."

"Why would I kill a man I never met? I am not a cold-blooded contract killer."

"But Lucio—"

Bagdesarian stopped him mid-sentence. "Let's stop right there." Leaning over with a forefinger in Bergman's face, he said, "First, I was thirteen when they murdered my grandfather on a Paris street. I never met my grandfather, and I wasn't in Paris when whoever murdered him."

"But you all but told me you hired the killer."

"Careful now, or Lucio will talk with you, and you don't want him talking to you. You can trust me on that."

Alan kept his eyes on Bagdesarian, looking for anything. "Are you saying you didn't hire your grandfather's murderer?"

"Let me *say* this as clearly as I can. I caution you to be

careful with the words that come out of your mouth. I did not kill my grandfather. Nor did I hire anyone to kill him. Nobody is going to take a contract from a teenager, still wet behind the ears." Bagdesarian focused on Bergman for confirmation he understood. "No one knows who killed the old man. It is an unsolved case. I have no idea who killed your friend in Texas. Lucio and I just returned from a trip to Easter Island. We met with some Chilean businessmen, and we talked of a new South American venture."

Alan relaxed a little. Lucio returned and gave a nod to Bagdesarian. "I had Lucio reserve a room at the Rendezvous for you. Go to the hotel. Raid the little refrigerator and get drunk. Get naked in the hot tub, I don't care. But leave now. I will meet you at the hotel's restaurant in the morning at nine. If you have calmed down, we can talk to your little heart's content. But we will not discuss me killing your Texas connection—or anyone else. Ever! Now leave."

Alan opened his mouth to talk. Nothing came out. Lucio, who had been standing at the table, took a step toward him. Bagdesarian raised his hand. "Mr. Bergman, we have said enough tonight. It is possible we have said too much. It's time for you to go."

Alan sat there for another moment. He realized there was nothing left to be said. He got up and headed to the Rendezvous and his room. He took his shoes off and lay on the bed, staring at the ceiling. He considered taking a shower and getting some sleep. But his mind would not unwind. Alan believed Lucio was going to pay him a visit during the night, making breakfast with Bagdesarian a moot point.

At three, with no visit from Lucio, Alan began to relax. He showered and climbed into bed and had just closed his eyes when a noise startled him. He opened his eyes to the bright sunlight. It was 8:15. The noise was the alarm on his phone. He had survived the night.

* * *

At 8:45, Alan opened his door to find Lucio standing there.

"Got a gun?" the man asked.

"No."

Lucio patted Alan down. "Had to make sure. Gonna make any more crazy accusations?" Lucio opened his coat to show Alan his gun.

"Bagdesarian said when you talk, people die. Tell me the truth. You are talking. Does that mean I am a dead man?" said a trembling Alan.

"Oh, I talk plenty and no one dies." Opening his coat again, Lucio continued, "It is a different story when Lucretia talks. When she talks, people die."

"Is she in a talkative mood?

"Na, she's got laryngitis." Lucio smiled as he escorted Alan to the restaurant.

* * *

Noticing Bergman was in the same clothes as the night before, Bagdesarian began, "Alan, my boy. You need to plan for contingencies. You look like a drunk fresh from the tank," and he smiled.

"Feel like I've been in the tank," Bergman replied and sat down.

"I have ordered breakfast for us. I have another engagement this morning and you have a flight to catch."

"Fine," said Bergman, taking a sip of coffee.

"Lucio did some checking. Yes, they shot your friend in a manner similar to my grandfather. Same two shots. Same caliber. It would not surprise me if it were the same gun."

"So?"

"No," said Bagdesarian, "I had nothing to do with your friend's murder. Yes, you are a person of interest because of some

98

foolish, harassing techniques you used to coerce your friend to sell his business."

"I followed what you taught me. The emails are untraceable."

"Don't care. You are a person of interest.

"I thought the emails would seal the deal," Alan started.

"They didn't. Seems your friend had already worked out a deal with some other guy. He owns the Cheyenne Ranch. Harold Ragsdale is his name. Ever meet him?"

"No," said Alan.

"Lucio confirmed your alibi is solid, and since you don't own a gun—"

"How? How do you?" protested Alan, but Bagdesarian cut him off.

"It's my business. My appraisal of the situation is you have nothing to worry about. Those stupid emails are just that, stupid emails." Bagdesarian took a bite of egg and a sip of coffee. "They may harass you, but they are not coming after you."

"You say it is your business to know. Do you know who did it? Who killed A.C.?"

"No," said Bagdesarian. "This is the second enigma I have encountered. Like with my grandfather, I cannot find the identity of the shooter. Whoever he is, this killer is very methodical. And good. Very good."

"I apologize for last night," Alan said in a quiet voice. "Life has become more than a little stressful in Texas."

"Let's finish breakfast. Lucio and I will take you to the airport. It is on the way to my next meeting. And next time you come to talk with me, bring an extra suit. You look like you are guilty as sin!"

Aware he had dodged a bullet, Alan forced a smile as he got out of the cab. He managed a casual salute. He thought, how stupid could he have been? Yes, the murder of A.C. and Bagdesarian's grandfather were similar. But what would Bagdesarian have gained with killing Mottola?

As he stood at the gate counter, he reached inside his pocket for his ticket. He felt another piece of paper in there. He handed the person at the gate his ticket and read the note. His heart missed a beat. It had four words, neatly printed. *Lucretia is talking again.* He did a three-sixty but saw nothing and boarded his plane.

CHAPTER 15

Two weeks after the first meeting, Carol Sager, Charlie Musselwhite, and Harold Ragsdale sat in the law office of Mitch Miller. Musselwhite shared stories of how he and A.C. first met and their friendship. The friendship and respect he earned in the community and his prowess at the billiard table. The meeting was cordial, and Carol relaxed.

Ragsdale cleared his throat, shuffled some papers in front of him, and began the most challenging segment of the meeting. "Miss Sager, I am happy you have been able to hear the chief and Mr Miller's fond memories of their friend, Anthony. Your father." He watched as the woman's face tensed. Then he began again slowly and deliberately. "Anthony. My buddy was a special man. Our friendship dates back over two decades. I am an only child, and I considered him to be the brother I never had. He, also, was an only child and shared the same sentiment."

The ease showed by Carol during the stories shared by the chief and Mr. Miller left. Instead, her features hardened. The smile was gone, and her eyes were drilling a hole into Ragsdale's face. As Musselwhite and Miller had told their stories, Carol had her hands clasped and resting on the table. Now, leaning back in her chair as if to distance herself from Ragsdale, she folded her arms and kept them tight against her body. When he understood there was no easy way to proceed, he plunged ahead.

"Your dad loved your mother and adored you. There is

nothing he would not do for either of you."

"Yeah. Right," Carol said in a caustic voice. "Tell me why he deserted us?"

"He didn't." Ragsdale held up a hand as Carol protested. "They did not divorce because your parents fell out of love. Nor was it because of any infidelity or drinking problem. Your dad loved you and your mother very much. It would not surprise me if your mother did not feel the same. The divorce was…" Ragsdale stopped as he searched for the right words. "As hard as it may be to accept, they divorced out of love."

Carol lowered her head and began shaking it. "No. No," she stammered. "He was a drunk." In time, she lifted her head, and Ragsdale saw the tears welling up inside. "He left my mother. Left her to raise me on her own. If he loved us so much, how come he never was a part of our lives? Never a letter, a card, or a phone call!"

"But he was."

"Stop! Stop! Stop!" said a now sobbing Carol. "Stop lying. My father didn't love me. He didn't love my mother. He didn't care about either of us. My father was a drunk, and he deserted us. That is the Anthony Mottola I knew!"

Miller got up and went to Carol. He put his arm around her in a consoling gesture. At first, she rejected the gesture, then leaned into him as she fought back the tears. Miller looked at each of the other men and settled on Ragsdale. "Gentlemen. I suggest this would be a good time to take a break." Everyone agreed. Ragsdale and Musselwhite left to give Carol time to catch her breath and regain control of her emotions.

"That was rough," said Musselwhite. "She had no clue?"

"No. As you will see, Anthony did not have a choice."

Musselwhite stood staring out of a window. "I am glad I am not you!"

* * *

Fifteen minutes later, they returned to the table. Blaine replaced Miller at the meeting allowing the lawyer to tend to other matters. Ragsdale took an envelope and handed it to Carol.

"Are you alright, Miss Sager?" asked a concerned Ragsdale.

"Yes. You are giving me a lot to digest in a short time. I grew up with one image of my father. An image I grew up hating. And." There was a pause. "And now you are telling me…" Again, she hesitated. "You are telling me mother lied to me? You are saying she lied to me. She lied about my father."

"I am not sure I would go that far," started Chief Musselwhite.

"Not go that far? What would you call it?" Carol was loud in her response. There was a shakiness in her voice. "My mother described my father as a mean drunk. And now I find out he wasn't."

"Miss Sager. Carol," began Ragsdale. "Yes, she lied to you in the beginning. When you were too young to appreciate things, she just never corrected it when you got older. I am sure she meant to tell you the truth. Life gets complicated. Life is complicated."

Struggling to maintain composure, she asked, "Do you have more pictures?"

Ragsdale picked up an envelope and handed it to her. "Here are your dad's favorites."

Carol took the envelope and removed the contents with a slight tremble in her hands. When she saw the contents, she gasped and put the photographs face down on the table. She looked at Blaine, then at Ragsdale with teary eyes for an explanation.

Without making eye contact, she said, "I, I, I don't know. I don't know if I can look at these."

"Our work, your dad's work, and my work became dangerous for ourselves. But, more importantly, it endangered our families, " said Ragsdale.

"How?"

"A hacker found and released our identities into the world."

"You were spies?"

"Not exactly," Ragsdale said. "But that is close enough. We worked for the government in clandestine roles. They are what the media likes to call 'black ops'. We were safe as long as no one discovered our true identities."

"And the hacker?" Carol asked.

"The hacker sold the list to various governments. This information included both our undercover names and our given names. One government said they were going after us. They said they were going to eliminate us." Ragsdale kept an eye on Carol. "And our families."

Carol's eyes widened, and she gasped and put a hand over her mouth.

"That is why your parents concocted the ruse of him being an abusive alcoholic. Your mother was against the idea, but your dad wouldn't budge. Nothing was more important to him than the safety of you and your mother. This idea became clear when they targeted one family on the list."

"Targeted, how?" Carol asked.

"They made two attempts on their lives and attempted to kidnap her daughter. The daughter was only eight."

"Her? That spy was a woman?" Carol asked in disbelief.

"Yes. One of the best. The mother got out and moved her family to the family's vineyard in Portugal. She dropped her American name. Her family has lived a quiet life in Lisbon."

She picked up the envelope's contents and asked, "And these pictures?"

"Most of them came from your mom, but some of them he took. He was there when you won state in soccer when you graduated from high school. He was at a few other events where there were enough people for him to blend in with."

"Why didn't he say something? Why didn't Mom—when she was dying?"

"Anthony loved you very much. Conditions were still unsettled. His foremost thoughts were for you and your mother.

He did not want to risk your safety."

"And Mom?"

"As for your mom, the cancer was aggressive. I don't think she had the strength to go through the ordeal. Remember, she was in a lot of pain in the end. There just was not enough time."

It was Musselwhite's turn to ask Ragsdale questions. "Did A.C. settle in our little town because he wanted to escape the big city rat race, or was that also a lie?"

"Yes, and no."

The chief looked at Ragsdale with raised eyebrows.

"Chief. It is not as simple as that," Ragsdale said.

"What do you mean? Either he settled to escape the big city or he didn't."

"Carol is the real reason he settled here."

She looked up from the pictures at the mention of her name.

"Then A.C. at least had an idea where his daughter was when he moved here," Musselwhite said.

"Yes. A.C. has always known where Carol was."

"Then why didn't he contact her?"

"Again. It is difficult to explain."

"What about the P.I. he allegedly hired?"

"There wasn't one. A.C. never talked to a P.I. and did not need to hire one. He always kept track of where his daughter was. So that wasn't the problem."

Carol looked up from the photographs and asked, "Then what? What was the problem?"

"Fear. He was afraid of how you might react. So he was working out a plan to reach out to you but also wanted it to be…well, accidental, I guess. He was hoping to one day move back into your life." Everyone was looking at Ragsdale. "Then his own cancer became an issue."

"Dad had cancer?" It was the first time Carol had referred to A.C. in a familial manner.

"Lung cancer," said Ragsdale. "It, too, was aggressive, and when he found out, he only had months to live."

"Why didn't he call? Or write?" asked Carol.

"I think he had a plan. He was coming out to Cheyenne to share it with me. But then, someone murdered him. He kept everything close to the vest, and I never had the details."

"Why didn't you call me?" Carol asked.

"That's a good question, Mr. Ragsdale," Musselwhite said. Then to Ragsdale. "Why didn't you tell us where his daughter was? Or how to contact her? You were aware we were looking for her."

"Didn't know," Ragsdale said. "We talked, and I understood he had worked out a strategy. But he kept everything private. After all we had gone through. He still couldn't expose his daughter."

"To what?" protested Musselwhite.

"Bergman," said Ragsdale.

"Bergman," Musselwhite and Blaine said in tandem.

Blaine finished the thought, "I knew he was involved."

"I don't think he was. A.C. was cryptic, but I got the impression Bergman didn't worry him, but someone Bergman knew." Ragsdale got quiet.

Blaine held up his hand in a timeout signal. "Guys, can we hold off discussing Alan Bergman's involvement until we have finished this meeting with Miss Sager?"

"If it involves my father, I think I would like to know."

Ragsdale looked at Blaine for help. Blaine spoke up and said, "Mr. Ragsdale is right. This is neither the place nor the time to discuss the Bergman angle. But, I assure you, Miss Sager, I will keep you informed as the investigation progresses."

Ragsdale took everyone through A.C.'s Triple M business holdings, his business relationship with A.C., and the trust account A.C. had set up for his daughter. Then Ragsdale handed Carol a business card. "When you are ready, call me. I will meet you at the Wells Fargo bank in Waco. That is where your dad set up the trust account. It is uncomplicated. You are the sole beneficiary."

"What is your role?" Carol asked.

"In the event that he died before he could connect with you, he made me executor of his estate and custodian of the funds."

"Custodian," asked Carol. "What does that mean?"

"It means I must find you and make you aware of the trust."

"What if I don't want it?"

"Anthony understood that was a possibility," said Ragsdale. "There are some contingency plans in that event. Do you want the trust?"

"I think so, but I am not sure," Carol said. "This meeting has been overwhelming. I came here with one understanding of my father. But what you all have shared tells me I was wrong. He is not the man I thought he was. I need time to think."

"I agree. It has been a lot to take in," said Ragsdale.

"Can Mr. Miller help me, or should I talk to another lawyer?"

The three men looked at one another. Then, after a pause, Musselwhite said, "Mr. Miller is a good man and an excellent attorney. I am sure if you wanted to talk to another attorney, he could give you several good lawyers to contact. But I believe your father would tell you to trust him."

The meeting lasted another fifteen minutes, then Carol left, saying she would contact Ragsdale when ready to look at the trust. Then the three men were alone.

CHAPTER 16

THREE DAYS AFTER they met with A.C.'s daughter Harry Ragsdale stood in a small interrogation room in the Limestone County Sheriff's Office.

"Take a seat," Blaine said as he entered the room.

"Will Chief Musselwhite be joining us?" asked Ragsdale.

"No. The city has turned the case over to us. The Sheriff's Office is investigating the fire at Triple M and Mr. Mottola's death. I am the lead investigator, so it's just you and me today."

As Ragsdale looked around at his surroundings, he asked, "Am I in trouble?"

"No. Not at all," reassured Blaine. "This is where I like to talk to people. It is away from the everyday business of the Office. This is not an interrogation room. That's downstairs."

Ragsdale sat back and relaxed.

"You mentioned Alan Bergman. What can you tell me about him?" Blaine asked.

"Like I said. Anthony mentioned him, but I can't say I ever met the man. I believe he has a business in a little town, Black something."

"Hollow. Black Hollow," added Blaine.

"That's it. Black Hollow. Beyond that, I am not sure what I can add."

"You said something about Bergman made A.C. shy away from even considering his offer to buy Triple M."

"Yes, and no."

Blaine looked up from his notepad and raised his eyebrows. While the meeting was being recorded, Blaine always had a pad. He made notes of items needing a follow-up.

"It wasn't Bergman that bothered Anthony," Ragsdale said. "It was someone near Bergman."

"Explain," said Blaine.

"As I said, we did a lot of work under the radar for the government."

"Yes, and you said someone released your identities."

"Well, Bergman may or may not be involved in Anthony's murder, but I doubt he is the hacker."

Blaine slid over a picture of Alan Bergman. "Ever see him?"

"Nope. Never had the pleasure."

Blaine took back the picture.

"A.C. said there was another man near Bergman," Ragsdale continued. "The man was at the table next to Bergman was and it was that man that caught Anthony's eye."

"Any idea why?" asked Blaine.

"The guy selling us out was a European, French, from what I was told. We were told he was a henchman for one of the mafia families. I don't recall anyone giving us a name. NSA had a picture of him, so we memorized what he looked like.

"Have you ever seen this guy?" Blaine showed Ragsdale another photo.

"Who is he?"

"Muscle for hire. Name is Lucio Dalla."

"No. That face I would know. What happened to us is always fresh in your brain."

"But A.C. did. At least, he thought he did."

"Listen, sheriff. What happened to us, to Anthony and me, cost us more than a bit of inconvenience. It put our lives in danger. Our families' lives were in danger. We may not have known his name, but we had a face." Ragsdale looked at Bergman's picture again. "That face we could never forget."

Blaine took a moment to review his notes and continued.

"You never saw this hacker?"

"No."

"But A.C. has?"

"That is my guess. I am confident it was not Bergman, but this hacker appeared to be next Bergman and his friend."

The interview continued for over an hour. Afterwards, Blaine walked Ragsdale out and assured him the Sheriff's Office would keep him informed. "We'll keep in touch. In the meantime, here is my card. Call me if you remember anything else."

* * *

Blaine knocked on Sheriff Hazelwood's door. Hazelwood motioned him in. He sat in a chair across the desk from his boss. "Well?" Hazelwood said. "Learn anything good?"

"Hard to say," said Blaine. "I understand there is a picture of the hacker that sold out Mottola and Ragsdale. Neither knew his name, but Mottola told Ragsdale he saw the man recently."

"Here in town?"

"I doubt it. But I am confident it was in Texas. It could have been Dallas, Austin, or Houston."

"What's the next move?" asked the sheriff.

"We need to have another talk with Bergman. From the very beginning, I sensed his involvement. Now, based on what Ragsdale said, I am certain."

"Good for the murder?"

"Not directly," said Blaine. "I feel his involvement in my bones. He is not a key player. But we need more information, and only Bergman may have the key."

"Well, bring him in."

"Can't right now."

"Why?" asked the sheriff.

"He is out of town. His phone goes to voicemail, and his car isn't at the house."

"Well, keep trying."

"Copy that," said Blaine and headed back to his office.

* * *

Sheriff Hazelwood slouched in a chair across from his deputy three days later. "Time for an update." He had his fingers steepled and his chin resting on the fingertips.

"Not much to report," began his deputy. "Bergman is still MIA. It appears he does not have a lot of friends in Black Hollow."

"Why do you say that?"

"No one knows where he is. Just as curious, no one seems to care. They describe him as *nice enough*, but we have found no one calling him a friend."

"What does your gut tell you?"

"Bergman is in the shadows of the story. He's like a photo bomber who won't go away. He always appears in the background but never seems involved in the picture."

"Think he did it?"

"You mean the murder and fire?"

The sheriff nodded.

"No. Not directly."

"Could have hired someone."

"Yeah, but I am unwilling to go down that rabbit hole. At least, not yet. I think Bergman knows something, only he isn't aware that he knows it."

"So. Where do you go from here?"

"We have the subpoenas for Mottola's phone and credit cards. So it is possible what we need will be there."

"What are you hoping to find?"

"According to Ragsdale, A.C. was at a restaurant where he noticed Bergman having dinner with another man. Perhaps that is where he recognized the hacker. However, he may not have been aware of the hacker's presence."

"How did A.C. recognize this ghost?"

Blaine flipped through some notes. "Here it is. Ragsdale said they had a picture but not a name. I think there was an informal hit put on this guy. He was a dead man if either of them saw him while working for the government."

"Interesting," the sheriff said. "And then?"

"So then, the two were civilians and couldn't go around killing people. Even actually bad people."

"True. But I am sure there were ways."

"To make him disappear?" Blaine finished the sentence. "They weren't criminals. They were not guns for hire. But you do raise a curious point."

"So, you put A.C. in a pleasant restaurant in a big city where he was conducting business. Then what?"

"Then we see if we can put Bergman in that restaurant."

"And find out who he was with."

Blaine snapped both fingers and pointed them at his boss. "Precisely."

"Well," Hazelwood said, as he climbed out of the chair. "Keep me in the loop."

"Will do," said Blaine. He leaned back in his chair and thought about what they had just covered. It was almost five when Blaine began shutting down for the day.

* * *

A clerk knocked on the doorframe as Blaine finished putting everything back into his file box. Motioning her in, she handed him a phone message. It was from Judee Sill, the medical examiner. He knew she was in San Antonio for a conference, and the note asked him to call her when he had a chance. Blaine looked at the note again. He smiled, then picked up the box and headed to the file room where the office kept active files. He stopped by Hazelwood's office to tell his boss he was leaving, but the sheriff had already left.

On the way home, he grabbed a Whataburger and soft

drink. Then he turned on the news and watched as he ate. When finished, he muted the television and called Dr. Sill.

CHAPTER 17

Blaine was on the phone when there was a knock. He glanced up and saw his boss at the door. "Bergman's home," he mouthed. Hazelwood gave a thumbs up. When he hung up, Blaine leaned back in his chair. His fingertips were on the edge of his desk.

"What's your game plan?" asked Sheriff Hazelwood. He was leaning against the doorframe, chewing on a toothpick. "Or are you going to wing it?"

The deputy was slow to respond. "My plan is to play it low-key. I want to give Bergman a reason to come in. After that, we can evaluate." The sheriff bounced his body off the doorjamb and took the visitor's seat in front of the desk. Blaine waited until his boss sat down and said, "I mean. There is no real reason for him not to come in and talk. He's not a suspect. Hey, he isn't even a person of interest."

"Are you sure?" asked the sheriff looking over steepled fingers. "He might see it differently. He may assume you are laying a trap for him and bring his lawyer."

"I considered that," said Blaine. "If I get Bergman here, I can convince him there is no danger of being charged, except for abusing that whole handlebar mustache thing." Both men laughed at that.

"Tell me the truth, Hal. What do you hope to get out of him?"

"Bart, I've narrowed the restaurant where A.C. ran into Bergman to the Lotus in south Austin. There was a record show at the Palmer. We can place A.C. in the restaurant. All based on what we recovered. The credit card receipts, and a few other things. I need to determine if our friend was there as well."

Hazelwood turned and looked out the window. He was silent for several minutes. Then, when his deputy turned back to him, he said, "The problem is friendship. What if the person was a friend? Bergman might not want to implicate him. Then you have only what you have now."

"Yes, that is a possibility. From my days as an M.P., I learned that it's not what you ask, but how you ask it. As the saying goes, this ain't my first rodeo. I've done this before and gotten what I wanted."

"And was your subject as skittish as our little man?"

"Worse. I had a soldier who murdered his girlfriend. I got him to confess before he realized it. Had it on tape."

"Yeah, but," Hazelwood interjected, "Bergman has a lawyer."

"So did that soldier. The lawyer was also involved. So, we nailed two birds with one stone." Blaine shrugged his shoulders in a who-knew gesture.

"Yes, but Bergman is not a viable suspect."

Blaine smiled. "I know. That will make it easier."

"OK," said the sheriff. "Just be careful.

"Copy that. I will be careful. Really careful."

The sheriff left, leaving Blaine to finalize his strategy.

* * *

Blaine opened the file at his desk and thumbed through pages of notes until he found what he wanted. He reached for the phone and dialed the number. A voice answered on the second ring.

"ABM, this is Alan. How can I help you?" The voice was professional, yet welcoming.

"Mr. Bergman, this is—"

"Yes, deputy," Bergman said, cutting Blaine off. "What do

you want now?" He replaced the welcoming tone with one of irritability. As an M.P. in the army, Blaine had to bring people in for questioning. Sometimes, it was when he interrogated a suspect, and others were witnesses. So Blaine understood, talking to law enforcement types was not always a pleasant experience.

The first time Blaine questioned Bergman, he was a suspect. Although the department cleared Bergman, Blaine knew the trauma of the experience lingered. He had to be careful, or Bergman would never cooperate. Adopting a conciliatory tone, he said, "I was hoping you could come into the office."

"Why?"

"There have been some fresh developments. As a result, we have some new questions, and we could use your help."

Bergman cut him off. "Am I a suspect, again?"

"No, you are not a suspect. As I said the last time we talked, we are confident you had nothing to with Mr. Mottola's murder or the arson of his business."

"Then what?"

Blaine remained calm.

"I understand you were in Austin in January. Ate at the Lotus restaurant. Ring any bells?"

"It is possible. I am in Austin a lot, and the Lotus is one of my favorite restaurants."

"It is possible you saw something. Something you didn't even know you saw." There was a pause. This was the tricky part. If Bergman did not consent to an in-person interview, the discussion would be over now. "Mr. Bergman, we believe Mr. Mottola was at the restaurant when you were there. So either something happened, or he recognized someone there. And I could use your help to figure out which it was."

"Didn't see him."

"That may be. But we still need to talk. And this needs to be a face-to-face conversation. I appreciate your hesitance. If you prefer, I guess I could stop by the store."

"Oh, no. You and your buddies have created enough problems for me. I'll come to you. When?"

Blaine celebrated missing the land mine. "Tomorrow, if you can. I should be here all day."

"How long is this going to take?"

Blaine relaxed and explained the meeting would be short. Only half an hour.

"What if I bring a lawyer?"

"Not a problem. Bring your lawyer along if it would make you feel more comfortable."

There was a pause, and Blaine was about to speak to make sure Bergman had not hung up. "OK, it is against my better judgment, and I'm still not sure I can trust you. But I will be there at ten."

"That's great. I'll see you and your lawyer at ten."

"No. I think I will come by myself. Just to be clear, my lawyer will be on speed dial. Especially if you have your buddies with you."

"Buddies?" Blaine asked.

"The sheriff and the chief. If they are in the meeting, we won't talk until my lawyer arrives."

Blaine said, "I promise it will be just the two of us." The deputy reconfirmed the time and disconnected. He made a note and went back to the Hazelwood's office. Blaine gave his boss a brief recap. The sheriff offered to sit in, but Blaine said no. He promised Bergman it would be just the two of them.

* * *

Blaine called his counterpart in the Travis County Sheriff's Office. They took a few moments and exchanged pleasantries.

"Got a situation, and I need your help," Blaine said.

"Shoot."

"Are you familiar with the Lotus restaurant?"

"My favorite," his friend said.

"It's a long shot, but some restaurants have cameras covering the bar and register areas."

"Becoming more and more common."

"What about the Lotus?"

"Not sure. Want me to check?"

"Yes. I am emailing you a photo of a guy associated with the Triple M murder and fire."

"Suspect?"

"No. But can't say the same for anyone he may have been with."

Blaine gave the Travis County Deputy the information, dates, and what he hoped to find. His friend said it would take a few days. In addition, he promised copies of the footage. If there were any.

* * *

"It's all set," Blaine told his boss. Sheriff Hazelwood stopped by on his way out of the office. "My contact in the Travis County Sheriff's Office will check if the Lotus has cameras in the building. I told him what I needed. He said it should take a week or two."

"And Bergman?"

"He will believe there are cameras, and I need to find out who was with him. To exclude them from whatever bothered A.C."

"Think he'll tell you who they are?"

"I think he will. Especially if he believes he is off our radar," said Blaine with a smile.

"Does it? I mean, does it get him out from under our radar?"

"He is now. I am not interested in him. Just his friends."

"When is he coming in?" asked Hazelwood.

"Tomorrow at ten."

"You won't have the camera info by then."

"No, but he won't know that. He will believe the Lotus has

cameras, and we have seen pictures."

As he turned to leave, the sheriff wished his deputy well and cautioned him again to be careful.

Blaine returned to his office, did a fist pump, and said to no one, "Gotcha."

CHAPTER 18

It was the last day of the Oklahoma Sooner Music Show. Vendors represented several states, Japan, England, and Germany. Bergman was loading his trailer when his phone rang. Although there was no caller ID, he recognized the number. He swiped the phone and held it to his ear. Before he could say anything, the voice on the other end said, "We need to talk."

"Sure, Ross. When and where?"

"What time do you close?"

"This show ended at 5:00. I should be back at my hotel by 6:30."

"Meet me in the lobby at 7:00. We'll have a late dinner at Campanella's."

"Sure, no problem." Bergman studied the phone for a second before putting it in his pocket.

* * *

It was after eight when Rob Campanella, owner of Campanella's, seated his guests. Bergman and Bagdesarian sat together while Dalla kept a close watch at a nearby table. Ross had Pasta 'Ncasciata with tomato sauce and Bergman had Pasta con Tenerami. As usual, Dalla limited his meal to breadsticks and water. Bagdesarian ordered a bottle of Nero de Avola.

The chatter during dinner was casual. They talked about everything and nothing. Ross seemed to enjoy himself while

Alan was trying to determine why Ross was in Oklahoma City. If it weren't for the record show, Bergman would not choose to be here. It is not a tourist destination. Alan was about to find out.

After the waiter cleared the dishes and refilled the wine glasses, Bagdesarian raised his glass in a silent toast to Bergman. "So, Alan. Tell me. How did the show go?"

"Very well," Bergman began. "I doubled my inventory, so my trailer heading back to Texas will be full."

"Was that your goal?" Bagdesarian was being more polite than interested.

"No. Not really. But Bud Ebsen had the booth next to mine. Unfortunately, he lost his wife earlier this year. They had been together for fifty years and doing record shows for the past ten. In his seventies, he decided to honor his wife and do one more show before calling it quits."

"And you helped him out."

"I guess so. I paid a fraction of what his booth was worth. I asked him yesterday what he wanted for his inventory, and he gave me a price. It was lower than I was about to offer, so I jumped at it. We closed the deal last night, and I combined the booths today."

"Aside from that purchase, how did you do?"

"About $4,500."

"Mostly credit card, I presume," said Bagdesarian before taking another sip of wine.

"You would think, but most of my transactions were cash. Of course, there are those big spenders who rely on credit cards. But most visitors come in to browse and make an impulsive purchase. Some come looking for that one obscure record or CD. Either way, they are always on a budget."

"CDs? People still buy those? You know, most newer cars don't even have a CD player."

"You're right. But these people don't care about streaming services. They want to have that piece of nostalgia in their hands. These people are serious and bring their portable record players, CD players. Even cassette players. I mean, these people are know their music. Then, there is the software. It will convert albums and cassettes to digital mp3 files, stored in the cloud and accessible from anywhere." Ross looked at his friend with skepticism. "I'm telling you, Ross, these folks are fanatics. There aren't any Blockbusters or Tower Music stores anymore. But every city of any size has a music store selling both old and new vinyl and CDs."

"What was the most expensive item at this show?"

"Nothing, really. there was not that need-to-have, one-of-a-kind item. At the last Austin Record Show, an Elvis Presley Christmas album sold for just over three grand."

"Three grand? What made it so special?"

"RCA in its hay day used colored vinyl to identify the targeted market. Green was country, red was classical. Black was everything else. The Elvis Christmas album sold to the public was on black vinyl. However, he had a handful pressed in the red vinyl. He gave these to family and friends for Christmas."

"How many?"

"I don't know for sure. Probably not more than five or six in total."

"Let's change the subject." Okay, Alan thought, here comes the real reason for the visit. "I hear our friendly deputy sheriff wants another sit down with you. Any idea what he wants?"

"Where did you hear that?"

"I have my sources. Is it true?"

"Yes," said Bergman and took a gulp of water.

"What does he want?"

"Not a clue." Alan felt his blood pressure rising.

"Are you still a person of interest?" Bagdesarian was swirling his wine and did not look at his guest.

"I don't see how. My alibi for the night of the fire is solid. And I don't have a motive. I mean, why would I destroy what I was trying to buy?"

"Am I in the picture?" Bagdesarian asked.

"Don't see how. I've never mentioned you."

"Good. See our deputy but take a lawyer."

"Lee Graham is coming with me. He's with Cashman & West out of Waco."

"Good. Keep me posted." The tone showed their meeting had concluded.

Alan stood was about to leave when he turned to Bagdesarian and asked, "Wait. You came up from Houston to Oklahoma City just to ask me what the sheriff wanted with me?"

Bagdesarian chuckled, "No, you're not that important. Lucio and I are flying to Chicago to see Justin Peroff, an old friend. His youngest girl is getting married. We had time so we thought why not come and see you. That okay with you? Alan thought for a moment, nodded, and left for his room.

* * *

Dressed in work boots, jeans, a western shirt, and a Stetson, Ragsdale blended in with the others in the waiting room. He carried a shoebox under his arm which he placed on the receptionist's desk.

"May I help you?" the receptionist asked. Her name badge identified her as Allin Travers.

Noticing her badge, he ignored her question and said, "Allin. That's a unique name."

Used to the comment, she smiled and said, "I usually go by Allie."

"Usually? Not all the time?"

"When I came to work, there was a doctor named Allie. So, I used my formal name to avoid confusion?"

Looking at the list of doctors on staff, he asked, "Allie, is the doctor still here?"

"Nah, she married and became a stay-at-home wife when her first child arrived." Looking around the visitor, she asked,

"What kind of animal do you have?"

"Oh, I'm sorry. No animal." Allin gave him a quizzical look. "I just need to see Dr. Sager. Is she available?"

"Dr. Sager is with a client right now. Who should I –"

"Harold Ragsdale. It's a personal matter; if she's too busy, I can come back another time."

"Mr. Ragsdale, let me see if she has time to talk to you." Allin disappeared down a hall. A few minutes later, she opened a side door. "Mr. Ragsdale?" He followed Allin down a hall with several doors. He presumed they were offices and storage rooms. Allin stopped at one with the name *Dr. Carol Sager, DVM*, on the door. "Dr. Sager asked me to have you wait here in her office. She said she would be right with you." Allin nodded, smiled, then closed the door.

Ragsdale read Carol's diploma from Texas A&M, and her vet's license. Then, he examined three photos of Carol with an older woman he presumed was her mother. When Carol opened the door, he was behind her desk looking at the photographs. "Mr. Ragsdale. So nice to see you again." Her voice was warm and friendly

Ragsdale smiled, moved from behind her desk, and the two shook hands. Then, nodding to the photographs, "Your mother?"

"Yes. Have a seat," and pointed to two chairs in front of her desk. She sat in her chair behind the desk. "What brings you to Montgomery?"

"I am still going through your father's stuff he stored at my ranch. I came across this" lifting the shoe box "and thought you might like to have it." He handed the box to her.

Carol set the box on her desk and opened it. "What is it?"

"I saw it was personal and thought you should have it."

Carol laid the box's contents on her desk. There were newspaper clippings, cards, photographs, and a stack of letters. She thumbed through the stack and saw her name on each sealed envelope.

"I guess those are letters he wrote, but never mailed. Anyway," pointing to the letters, "they are yours."

In a soft voice, she looked up at her visitor and said, "Thank you."

They visited for a few more minutes. "I'm sorry to cut this short, but I have a rancher with a lame horse. Can you stick around, and maybe we can have dinner?"

"I'd love to, but I am headed to Houston. I wanted to get these to you, and this seemed a perfect time. Come up to Cheyenne Ranch sometime. We'll have that dinner and do some riding."

"Thanks. I may take you up on that if I get a free weekend." Carol walked her guest to the clinic's door. She said, "Mr. Ragsdale, thank you for taking the time to bring the box to me. I appreciate it" She held out her hand.

He ignored the gesture and touched the brim of his hat and gave a short nod. "My pleasure." She watched him get into his truck and drive away.

CHAPTER 19

WHEN BERGMAN AND Graham arrived, Blaine showed no emotion. The interview went better than expected. Blaine learned that Bergman had met with a business associate, Ross Bagdesarian, and his partner, Lucio Dalla. Dalla was at a separate table. Bergman could not say why the man sat at another table. Other than to say, it was the custom. Whenever Bergman and Bagdesarian met to discuss business, Lucio was always near, but never part of the discussion.

Blaine heard from his contact in Travis County and learned the Lotus did not have cameras. However, the hostess was accommodating. She remembered both Bergman and Mottola being there before. She remembered Bergman because of his mustache. The waitress smiled and said her father had a similar one. She also remembered A.C. because of his looks.

Blaine chose not to interview anyone at the restaurant. Instead, he got what he needed from Bergman. Because he had met with two Europeans, Blaine reached out to Interpol. Blaine had completed the online information when his phone rang.

"Limestone Sheriff's Office, Blaine speaking."

"Don't you ever read your messages?" It was Judee Sill, the medical examiner who did A.C.'s autopsy. There was an undertone of frustration.

"Yes, I read my messages. I even returned your call."

"I didn't get it," said Sill.

"Your voicemail was full. Don't you ever dump your old

messages?”

“Forget that,” she said. “Can you come to San Antonio tomorrow?”

“I’ll have to clear it with Bart, but I think I can make it.”

“Tell Sheriff Hazelwood the trip will give the Triple M incident a whole new look.”

“Pray, tell. What is happening?”

“I am at an international forensics symposium. There is someone here you will want to meet,” Sill said with excitement. “He is an inspector with Interpol.”

“You got to be kidding!” said a surprised Blaine. “I just sent an information request to Interpol.”

“Well, I’ll bet he can give you what you want without waiting days or weeks.”

“We are at the Hotel Valencia Riverwalk,” Sill continued. “The hotel is hosting the symposium. Get the sheriff to let go of some cash and get down here. Pronto!”

Blaine found his boss at the coffee machine. He shared what Judee Sill had said and received the thumbs up. “Fill out the paperwork before you leave. That or the trip will be on your dime.”

“Copy that,” said Blaine and headed back to his office. Fifteen minutes later, he was in a sheriff’s department black Tahoe and headed south. The traffic was light. Blaine felt sure he would be there in time for dinner with Sill and her new Interpol friend.

* * *

The Hotel Valencia was along San Antonio’s famed Riverwalk. There were a few guests on the patio but would become overflowing when night fell over the city. When Blaine checked in they gave him his key and a note from Sill. *Meet me at the restaurant at 5:30.* Blaine rode the elevator to the tenth floor, found his room, and settled in. He had an hour before he had to meet with Sill and her inspector from Interpol. He spent the time reviewing the case file.

* * *

With an air of excitement, the deputy arrived early and waited for his M.E. at the entrance to the restaurant. Sill and the inspector from Interpol were late. It was close to six when he spotted his M.E. accompanied by a middle-aged gentleman in a gray suit. The man had thick, dark hair and a gray shirt. It was a shade lighter than the suit. He was clean-shaven and had a black leather attaché case in his left hand. When Judee saw Blaine, she waved and hastened to reach him.

They liked each other and occasionally saw each other socially. Today, Judee's smile said she was glad to see her deputy. The two were professional when they met. Sill introduced her new friend, and they followed the hostess to a table. It was on the window-side of the restaurant. Sill's lab had no windows, and she always enjoyed a window seat. There she could look out into the world.

"Inspector Dutronc, is it? Dr. Sill tells me you are with Interpol," Blaine said, breaking the ice.

"Yes, but please call me Jacques. I've been with Interpol for over ten years. It's interesting, and I can travel." He had a deep voice, with a thick French accent. Hearing the accent reminded Blaine of the Belgian singer Jacques Brel. Was the inspector French or Belgian? Jacques brought Blaine back to reality saying, "Judee has been sharing information about your murder victim."

Blaine twinged at the familiarity in the man's voice. It caught him off guard and created a sense of irritation. He knew there was no basis for his anger. Blaine thought and then discarded the notion of jealousy. Around the crime scenes, they worked together. Most people called her by her last name, or Dr. Sill. He was the only one among their cohorts to call her Judee. And only when they were alone and out of earshot of those around them. "And I understand you have something to share." Blaine smiled and hoped his voice did not betray what he felt.

"We have had several similar killings. Without the fire, of course."

"Similar?" Blaine focused on the murder.

"The first occurred decades ago. Someone shot an old man in Paris—twice."

"One in the chest and one in the head?"

"Same as yours. Except they didn't burn the old man. However, they stuffed a note in his mouth."

Blaine's curiosity moved up a notch. "A note? What did it say?"

"C'est pour ma mère, C'est pour prendre ma jeunesse."

"I'm sorry, inspector. My French is a little rusty," said an apologetic Blaine.

"The note read, *This is for my mother, This is for taking my youth*," said Dutronc.

"Who was the old man?" asked Blaine.

"As far as we can tell, his name was Auguste Chevalier."

"You're not sure?"

"In many small towns, women gave birth at home. Following tradition, they recorded the name in a family Bible. Not all families followed this tradition. We believe he was born in the early to mid-1920s. Back then, births were not required to be registered. So, you appreciate our dilemma."

"Well then, how did you come up with the name?" Blaine wanted to know.

"They shot him in an industrial area of town. There were apartments on the next street over. We learned he lived in one of those apartments. While canvassing the neighborhood for witnesses, we learned in what apartment he lived. The name on the mailbox read Auguste Chevalier. So, that is what we acted on."

"Works for me. Whose mother was killed and whose youth

was stolen?"

"That, my friend, we have never learned. They shot Chevalier as he walked his dog.

"Was he alone?" asked Blaine. Judee ignored the conversation. She and the

inspector had discussed the case earlier. She took the time to enjoy a favorite hobby. People watching.

"Yes, except for his dog. After being shot, he fell on the dog's leash. The dog never left his side. "

"And the time of death?"

"We believe they shot him around midnight."

"Why then?"

"Simple. The weather. It rained after midnight. The streets were wet."

"But the pavement underneath the body was dry," said Blaine.

"Precisely. A shopkeeper opened up. He found the dog sitting by a pile of clothing. This was around six. He walked to the dog and discovered the body. He called the local police. After two or three weeks, the investigation hit a dead end."

"You were with the police back then? Your case?"

"Yes and no," Dutronc began. "I had recently joined the police. My beat was on the other side of town. Besides, it was a case for detectives, not a new neighborhood officer. What you Americans call a beat cop."

Sill sat patiently, listening while the two men talked. Dutronc had explained this to her twice during the symposium, and she was thankful when the food arrived "I'm famished. Let's eat!" Judee said. Everyone enjoyed typical Tex-Mex faire and filled the meal with small talk.

Touching Blaine's arm, Judee excused herself to return phone calls and messaged which had accumulated during the day. Walking by, she let her hand brush Blaine's shoulder. She bent over and said, "Meet me on the patio, say about ten. We can have a drink and I'll bring you up to date with what I've learned."

"What about Jacques?" Blaine asked, pointing to the other man.

Dutronc brushed off the question. "I am meeting with my colleagues for some entertainment. This is our last night in town. My flight doesn't leave until tomorrow afternoon. We have time tomorrow to talk. I will fill you in then mon ami."

"Great. I'm in room 1010. Call me when you're ready," Blaine said watching Dutronc leave. Blaine enjoyed the company but felt disappointed the good stuff would have to wait until tomorrow.

CHAPTER 20

JACQUES WAS WAITING in the hotel restaurant when Judee and Blaine arrived. He signaled, and they joined him at the table. Dutronc remembered Sill's preference and sat at a window table. Blaine held the chair for Judee before taking a seat between Judee and Jacques. Jacques rose from his chair as the couple took their seats. He nodded at Judee and shook Blaine's hand.

Jacques raised his cup as a toast and said, "Good morning, Judee. I trust you and the deputy had an enjoyable evening." Blaine felt that twinge of jealousy again at the familiarity of Dutronc's greeting.

The waitress arrived and took the breakfast orders from the newcomers. "I'm sorry," said Jacques as the two looked at him. "Sorry, I've already eaten. Out late. I needed to eat to get my energy levels up. I should have waited, but…"

"Nonsense," said Judee. "We're fine if you don't mind if we talk and eat at the same time."

"No problem," said Dutronc.

"So," Blaine started, "has Dr. Sill filled you in on our case?"

"With great detail, I'm afraid," said Jacques. "It is good I ate before you arrived. I don't think I could eat and relive what happened to this poor man." He appeared to shudder as he took a sip of coffee.

"Dr. Sill said you had some information that might be helpful."

"There are several unsolved cases where the unsub shot the

victim twice."

"Once in the heart and once in the head?"

"Oui," said Jacques. "But no one burned them." He reached for his coffee cup and then switched to his water. Looking at them watching him, he said, "Sometimes, water is all I can handle." He moved his dirty dishes to the unoccupied seat and pulled out an envelope. He handed it over to Blaine. "These are for you. I have already given Judee a copy."

There were seven photographs. Some were black and white, and others were in color. The back identified the cities where the murders took place. *Troyes, Fr.; Saint Cloud; Fr., Assisi, Fr.; Padova/Padua, It.; El Escorial, Sp.; Almada, Port.* Then, holding up a black-and-white photo of a man near a dog. "This one," Blaine asked.

"Oh, that one is Auguste Chevalier. As far as we know, it was the first."

"Is that the one with the note inside the mouth?" Judee wanted to know.

"Yes."

"Did any of the others have any notes or anything else remarkable?"

"Until your Mr. Mottola, that was the only unique one. So, therefore, we believe it was the first. If there were others before that, we haven't found them." Blaine continued studying the pictures.

"Any leads?" asked Judee.

"They are what you call cold cases. We are out of leads."

Blaine asked the inspector, "What is the common denominator?"

"Except for Chevalier, the other victims had dealings with the Cosa Nostra. What you Americans call the mafia or the mob."

Judee asked, "Do you know which one?"

"Not for sure. The best guess is a new family, the Bagdesarians. Headed by a ruthless upstart, Ross Bagdesarian. Some assume it is his mother mentioned in the Chevalier note."

"Why?" Blaine's curiosity was up.

"His mother was Scottish, his dad Russian. There was a nasty divorce, and they awarded the mother full custody of a young boy. The mother died a few years later. The authorities found little Ross in Russia living with his father."

"Interpol?"

"No. Interpol was never involved."

"Was she, the mother, shot twice?"

"No. I haven't seen the file myself, but I believe they strangled her. This happened long before I was a policeman."

Blaine examined each photograph, one by one, and then passed each to his medical examiner. Other than the two bullet holes, the pictures revealed little. They were all men, but some were young while others were old. Some were city killings, and they found others in fields. They shot one in their bed. Other than to confirm their murder was not the first, neither Blaine nor Judee saw much use in the pictures.

After examining all the photos, Blaine asked, "What can you tell me about them? I'm not sure how they help my case."

Jacques put the pictures back in his folder and set it aside. He folded his hands and put his hands on the table. Then he studied his hands before raising his head, saying, "Two things. First, they are related to your case because of the method of killing.

There are no other killings with the specific M.O. said Jacques.

"What?" asked Blaine. It is not that uncommon for someone to be shot twice.

"Yes," continued Dutronc. "We have determined the chest shot was first. Still alive but unable to defend themselves, the victims are very much aware the head shot is coming."

"That can't be fun," mused the deputy.

"No. We believe these killings are associated with the Bagdesarian family. I believe you talked with Alan Bergman."

"Yes. We cleared him and he is not a suspect."

"But he is a known associate of Bagdesarian. Keep searching. I am sure you will find a connection." He retrieved the folder and opened it again.

"This one is Alfred Satie. The department believes he was a lieutenant in the family and they shot him while in bed. The investigators found a witness. No one reported hearing a gunshot."

"Where was this?" Judee asked.

"He had an apartment in Troyes, a small city near Paris. The word on the street is Satie was skimming money off his collections. The Cosa Nostra families do not tolerate skimming. No one is sure, but—"

Blaine interrupted, "he was an enforcer?"

"From what I hear, he was rather ruthless in his dealings. Satie was the prime suspect in several assaults. He was a bone breaker, but one client was not so fortunate. Satie murdered him."

Dutronc laid down the following two photos. "Bruno Ughi is the color photo. Sergio Galli is black and white. They were bound and weighted down in the Arno River in Florence. We understand Sergio was part of the family's inner circle. Accountant?"

"And Ughi?" asked Blaine.

"Mystery. Since they were bound together before being thrown into the river, we assume he was also part of the family. But we had never heard of him until we fished him out of the river. We found nothing connecting the two."

Blaine picked up the photo of Ughi again. "You are missing something. I mean, you don't double-tap a civilian, tie him to a problem employee and dump both in the tank unless there is a connection. So, what do the Florence authorities say?"

"I agree. Sergio is from Prado, a suburb of Florence, but Ughi is from Padua. That is near Venice. We couldn't place him in Florence before he went swimming. A similar story for

Sergio. No one remembers ever seeing him in Padua."

"They might have agreed to meet at a neutral site between the two cities," suggested the medical examiner.

"That's our working theory," said Dutronc. "Ughi must have been a family member who kept him busy elsewhere. So rather than hunting them down, the two met, and the family got a two-for-one special."

Dutronc spread the remaining pictures on the table the way one would display tarot cards. Next, he identified the remaining faces. "This is Jean Poulenc. He worked in the Versailles area." Not getting a response, he laid the next one on the table. "This is Andres Torres from El Escorial near Madrid. The last is Daniel Almeda from Alameda, outside of Lisbon."

"And the connection?"

"You mean besides the two bullets?"

Blaine nodded.

"None that we have found. The theory is the Bagdesarians have ties in both France and Italy. But, we don't know of any family business conducted in Spain or Portugal. So, another dead end."

"I still say you are missing something," Sill said, shuffling the pictures around.

"That, my dear Judee, is obvious. Whoever murdered these men did it out of sight and hearing. We are operating with a blindfold."

"I have one question," said Sill. "OK, two questions. Is the chest wound before the head wound in each case?"

Dutronc nodded in the affirmative.

"And was the same gun used for each murder?"

"Excellent question. Because the weapon was a small caliber, they retrieved bullets from each body. That is the one thing tying them together. In addition, they used the same gun each time. This suggests the murderer is the same for all. That includes both the double murder in Florence and the first murder of Chevalier in Paris."

"Most of the murders took place in smaller towns. Do you think this was by design or coincidental?"

"Mr. Blaine, do you believe in coincidences?"

"Not where murder is involved."

"Neither do I. As your beautiful colleague has reminded me twice, we are missing something."

At the word *beautiful,* Blaine looked up and saw a smiling Dutronc. Not that his medical examiner was unattractive. It made Blaine dislike Dutronc that much more.

With the business at hand settled, the three relaxed and shared travel experiences. Blaine's phone vibrated, and he looked at the screen. "Boss," is all he said and got up from the table to take the call in private. Boss said to come home.

"Now?" asked Sill.

"When the boss calls, you don't ask questions. So, I'm on the road tonight."

* * *

After picking up the tab for the meal, Blaine went back to his room. Later, Sill and Dutronc left the restaurant and headed to the concierge. "You like your deputy, don't you?"

"Huh?"

"You two are," he paused, searching for the word he wanted, "an item?" Dutronc smiled and enjoyed his companion's embarrassment.

"What? Me? Hal? No, we are friends. We have a professional relationship."

"I don't think Deputy Hal sees it that way." Dutronc studied his companion for a reaction. She tried, but the blush was there.

"I need to take care of some last-minute things. You have a safe trip home, and we will talk when I get back to Paris. No?"

"Jacques, it has been nice meeting you. We both thank you for your help. You have a pleasant flight home." Being familiar with the continental custom, she kissed him on both cheeks and then turned and left.

Dutronc watched her walk away and whispered, "Deputy, you are one lucky guy." Then he turned to the concierge and began making his arrangement for the flight back to Paris.

138

<h1 style="text-align:center">CHAPTER 21</h1>

IT HAD BEEN two weeks since Blaine, Sill, and Dutronc met in San Antonio. The package Dutronc promised arrived on Friday. Today, Saturday, was a quiet day in the office, and Blaine was in the conference room next to the records room. It was his day off, and he was confident no one would come looking for him.

The package was still unopened, and Blaine placed it on the table and opened the box. He placed his YETI with hot coffee on the table next to his cell phone. Blaine removed the contents with the package opened, put the box on the floor, and sat down. He grabbed a yellow legal pad and began writing.

1.   *If Bergman wanted to buy Mottola's business, why kill the man?*
2.   *Why the fire? To hide the murder or? Blaine let the thought fade away.*
3.   *How is Ragsdale involved?*
4.   *Bagdesarian?*

As much as he tried, Blaine could not make sense of either A.C.'s brutal murder or the torching of his business. Sheriff Hazelwood, Chief Musselwhite, and Blaine spent many hours discussing the case without drawing conclusions. There was plenty of time, and Blaine was in no rush to go through the box's contents. He posted the gruesome picture of A.C.'s burned remains on the corkboard. He moved the stack of case files to have a clear space in front of him and picked up the first file from the stack.

> *A shopkeeper discovered Auguste Chevalier, sixty-seven, shot to death on the Rue de la Mer in the early morning hours of 17 September 1982. Chevalier's dog remained at his side, the leash pinned between the old man's body and the sidewalk. There was one GSW in the upper left chest and a second in the forehead. The Medical Examiner estimated the time of death to be between midnight and one. The M.E. believed the chest shot was first. It was a kill shot, and Chevalier would have bled out within minutes. Because of the bleeding, Chevalier did not die from this shot. The headshot would cause immediate death. This wound had minimal bleeding, and the examiner determined this to be the proximate cause of death. The detective on the scene discovered a foreign object in the mouth of the deceased. There were no witnesses. Chevalier's neighbors described him as pleasant, but kept to himself.*

Blaine took a 3x5 headshot, added it to the board, and returned to the files. Convinced there was nothing more to be gained, he set the first file aside and picked up the next one.

The notation on the back read: *Alfred Satie, Troyes. Found in his bed, shot twice. The first shot was in the chest, and the second was a close-quarter headshot. The Medical Examiner used bleeding patterns to determine whether the headshot came last. The deceased was a known associate of the Bagdesarian family and had been dead at least 48 hours before they discovered the body. His doctor called the family when Satie missed an appointment. When questioned, the doctor showed the missed appointment was unusual. Satie was always ten minutes early. Concerned, the family asked a neighbor to check on him. When they could not arouse Satie, they found the door unlocked and entered the apartment. The neighbors noted smelling something like rotting meat. The bedroom door was closed, and they discovered the body when they opened the door. Nothing appeared to be missing, according to the investigators. The victim's watch and wallet, with several hundred francs, remained on the dresser.*

There was no date on the photo, so Blaine reviewed the file. He found the date of death was ten years to the day they shot Chevalier. Blaine noted Troyes is a suburb of Paris and wondered if Dutronc was involved. He was no longer a rookie beat cop.

"Come on, Freddy, tell me something I can use to find your killer," Blaine said out loud in a harsh whisper.

Organized crime was a primary interest of Interpol, and Blaine found what he wanted on the last page of the file. The Paris police invited Interpol, and Jacques Dutronc was the inspector assigned point. Blaine understood this made Dutronc the go-to guy at Interpol and made a note on his legal pad to call Dutronc.

* * *

"Jacques, Hal Blaine here. Have I caught you at a bad time?"

"I've got a nice red Bordeaux, and I'm sitting on the balcony looking at a beautiful sunset. But I'll pull myself away from the view for you, my friend."

"I'm sorry. What time is it?"

"It is 1900." Blaine forgot about the time difference.

"I'm so sorry to intrude on your evening. Should I call back in the morning?"

"No, this is fine. It's just me and the sunset. Now, if I had a beautiful woman with me…" Dutronc let the sentence die without completion.

Blaine ignored the sarcasm. "I'm looking over the files you sent. Thank you. I hope they give us something to work with."

"Fresh eyes are always welcome. What do you want?"

"I am looking at the Alfred Satie file and notice you were

the inspector."

"Yes. This was my first case after joining Interpol. It is still open. It remains a cold case."

Blaine did not respond to the cold case reference. "I see your M.E. put the date of death two days before they found him."

"I'd have to check my notes, but that sounds correct."

"That puts it ten years, to the day, after someone shot Chevalier. Any connection?"

"Judee said you were good." Dutronc smiled as he called Dr. Sill by her first name. His custom was to call a colleague by their last name. However, the inspector wanted to get under Blaine's skin. Dutronc wanted to see what reaction he would get. It disappointed him when he got none.

"So, what conclusion did you draw?"

There was silence, and Blaine thought maybe he had lost his call. Then Dutronc said, in slow and deliberate tones, "I recognized that irony. The only clue we had was that."

"Interpol?"

"Yes," Dutronc confirmed. "Interpol, and the Paris Police. We found a connection between Satie and Bagdesarian but could not tie Satie or Bagdesarian to Chevalier."

"You mentioned you believed the youth in the note might be Bagdesarian. Any confirmation?"

"Not directly, and especially not then."

"But now?" asked Blaine.

"Back then, we had two murders a decade apart with the same M.O. We operated on the assumption it was a Parisian thing."

"Then how did Interpol get involved?"

"The Paris Gendarmes. They connected the murders to Bagdesarian and brought us in."

With Dutronc on the line, Blaine took a few minutes to review the file.

"Blaine, you still there?"

"Sorry, Jacques. I just wanted to check something."

In a relaxed tone, Dutronc asked, "Find anything exciting? Like a smoking gun?"

"I don't know about smoking, but I am curious. Did your lab gurus check the bullets from each?"

"Another reason to believe it was local."

"So, they matched?"

"The same gun fired the bullets. It doesn't mean it was the same person, but it doesn't rule out that possibility."

"What about the others?" Blaine asked.

"The shooter, or shooters, used the same gun to commit the murders. That coincidence justified Interpol's involvement.

"I don't believe in coincidences," deadpanned Blaine.

"Neither do I."

"Look, Jacques. I've taken up enough of your time tonight."

"Who cares? The sunset is long gone."

"Sorry, old pal.

"Forget it, il y a toujours demain, n'est pas?"

"And that means?"

"There is always tomorrow, right?"

"Well, enjoy your Bordeaux, and we will talk again soon."

"Bonnne nuit, mon ami." And the line went dead.

* * *

"And you too, my friend. Blaine closed his phone and the file. The deputy stood, stretched, and studied the board. He looked at his watch and realized he had been reading files for four hours. He needed a break and headed to Mimi's, a hole-in-the-wall café. Mimi's had the best chicken and waffles in the area. Blaine figured that combination would be a perfect way to recharge his batteries.

As he was driving his canary-yellow Camaro, Blaine's phone vibrated. A message from Judee popped up. *Come up for air and meet me at the usual.* A smiley emoji ended the message. He backed out of his slot behind the Sheriff's Office, noticed that the sheriff was not there, then headed for *the usual*, as Judee had called Mimi's.

CHAPTER 22

BLAINE REACHED FOR the door at Mimi's and stopped. At the table with Judee were Chief Musselwhite and Sheriff Hazelwood. So much for a quiet lunch with his M.E. Blaine did not find the newcomers unwelcome, merely unexpected. He opened the door, smiled, waved at the trio, and walked to the table. He sat in the empty seat across from the medical examiner.

The sheriff looked at his deputy. "Surprised?"

"Nah," said Chief Musselwhite. "Disappointed."

Judee was quiet as she examined the menu.

"What?" exclaimed Blaine. "No. Neither." He glanced at one and then the other. No one believed him.

"Well, I am," said Sill. "Surprised, that is. I knew Hal was working this morning but thought you two," pointing at Hazelwood and Musselwhite, "we're off on a fishing trip."

"Maybe we are. It depends on what you're fishing for," said Musselwhite.

"Precisely," added Hazelwood, then the two of them laughed.

"Well, I'm famished," said Blaine and picked up a menu. "Have y'all ordered, or were you waiting for me to provide the entertainment?"

"No, and no," said Hazelwood. "The three of us got here at the same time and Sill said you were on the way. We waited for you before ordering. Any complaints?"

"Not on my part." Blaine looked at Judee and received confirmation.

"Besides," said Hazelwood, "the entertainment was lame." He and the chief shared thumbs up.

Musselwhite signaled the waitress, who took their drink and meal orders. The banter was friendly and lighthearted while waiting for the meal to arrive. Hazelwood and Musselwhite discussed the pros and cons of the area's various fishing holes. Blaine and Sill exchanged an occasional glance and listened but without enthusiasm. Sill was a city girl. Blaine had not done enough fishing to qualify as an expert on anything.

With lunch over, the table cleared, and beverages refreshed, Hazelwood asked Charlie about his staffing situation.

"It is getting better," he said. "Got Richard Starkey from the Azusa Police Department in California."

"Kind of a far reach, ain't it?"

"Not really. Richard came to me right out of the academy, then his parents got sick. His dad developed some type of dementia, then his mother got cancer. His father died two or three years ago. Then, six months ago, Richard's mother passed. He's an only child and heard we were looking for an experienced officer. He'll be back in Texas in two weeks."

"What about that other position?"

"Michael Love just graduated from the academy. He is going through orientation now."

"And your baby machine?" teased Hazelwood.

"Darlene is Michael's sister-in-law, married to his older brother. She is due back in about a month."

"You will have to contend with two Loves. What about your last-name only policy?"

The chief laughed, "Yeah. Need a new policy. Since the ranks are different, I could use the rank and the last name." Musselwhite took a large sip of coffee and set the cup down. "Oh, well. I have a few weeks before I need to worry about it."

Everyone tried to avoid the elephant in the room and sat in an uneasy silence.

###

"What? Who is Lennie Briscoe?" Judee asked, looking at the chief.

"An old TV Detective," said Hazelwood. "He's also dead."

"The actor may be, but not the character," said Musselwhite.

"Why be some television detective?"

"Always in a suit, never fired his weapon. And he always got his man. Plus, he worked one case at a time." The chief frowned. "I've got two homicides open, three B&Es, two arsons, and I am short on help."

"For me," said Hazelwood, "I'll take Danny Reagan. Both the actor and the character are very much alive. He has an attitude and a cute partner, and he always gets his man. And like Briscoe, he works one case at a time."

Everyone smiled, then their attention turned to Blaine.

"What about you, buddy boy?" Everyone looked at Hal.

"Sam Hannah. Hands down."

"Why?" everyone asked.

"He's way cooler than either of yours," Blaine replied, pointing to Hazelwood and Musselwhite. "He has a badder attitude than Reagan, and he has THE car."

Hazelwood laughed. "You're too short, skinny, and hairy to be him."

"What?" Judee asked in surprise.

"The rapper L.L. Cool J. plays the character. He is a lot taller than me," explained Blaine, "and he is bald. He shaves his head."

"And the skinny part?" asked Hazelwood.

His deputy explained, "Sam works out a lot. He has muscles on top of muscles. And drives a Dodge Charger."

"You know, your yellow bird is pretty nice," Judee confided referencing Blaine's canary yellow Camaro.

Everyone was looking at the M.E. "And who does the lady choose to be like? Maura Isles?" It was Hazelwood posing the question.

"Or perhaps Loretta Wade," suggested Musselwhite.

"First, I could never show up in a tight skirt, revealing

blouse, and stiletto heels to process a crime scene. I'd rip the skirt or fall over."

As he failed to stifle a laugh, Hazelwood said, "I'd pay to see that."

Sill shot him a look. "Miss Loretta doesn't do much. No, I'd like to be Abby Sciuto." Sill paused, made eye contact around the table, and concluded, "Yup. Abby it is."

"What? She isn't even a medical examiner," protested Musselwhite.

"True. But look at her toys. Abby has more toys in her little lab than any lab in Texas. Possibly in the whole U.S."

Hazelwood said, taking a last sip of coffee and wiping his mouth, "This has been fun, but the fish are calling. Come Monday, we will all have cases to solve."

"And more than one," added Musselwhite.

Sill turned to Blaine, "How's it going down in the dungeon?"

"I am making headway. It's slow, but I'm getting a clearer picture of everything.

"Any suspects?"

"Sure. Anyone with a twenty-five-caliber handgun they've kept for decades?"

"All kidding aside," said the sheriff. "Any suspects on your radar?"

"There are four names with ties to some victims. However, we can tie no one to all of them."

"Who are they?" asked the chief.

"Bergman is the only one associated with the first murder—Chevalier in Paris. The most common theory is he is the youth mentioned in the note stuffed in the victim's mouth. The only other murder I can tie him to is Mottola. And that is a stretch."

"The others?" pressed Musselwhite.

"Ross Bagdesarian and his henchman, Lucio Dalla. I believe they are associated with an upstart mafia family. I think the killings are consistent with mob hits."

"Even A.C.?" asked Musselwhite.

"It has all the earmarks of a mob hit."

Sill asked, "Was A.C. associated with the Cosa Nostra?"

"Not as far as I have discovered. His murder is consistent with the murders in Europe. The ones Dutronc told us about. But it doesn't feel right. I have found nothing to link A.C. with any mob activity.

"So," said Hazelwood, "you are focusing on this Bagdesarian guy?"

"Yes. He is elusive. I am trying to put him in the vicinity of the killings. So far, nothing."

"OK," said Sill. "So, who's the last one?"

"Your friend." Blaine watched his medical examiner for a reaction.

"My friend?" said a confused Judee Sill.

"Your Frenchman, Jacques Dutronc."

"He is Interpol," protested Sill.

"Still, other than the Chevalier killing, he is the only one." Blaine paused for emphasis. "And I mean the ONLY one whose name comes up with every murder."

"What about Mottola?" asked the sheriff.

"Except him, at least not yet," admitted Blaine.

"Do you expect his name to come up?" asked Sill.

"He is an inspector with Interpol, and Interpol keeps tabs on organized crime in Europe. Finding his name with the murders in Europe is not unexpected," explained Blaine.

"But you expect his name to come up. To be linked, in some way, to the Triple M thing?"

"I wouldn't say I expect it." Blaine took a sip of coffee and concluded, "But it would not be a total shocker either."

Musselwhite asked, "Think he's the killer?"

"Don't know," answered Blaine. "I assume the unsub is still in the wind. I am assuming Dutronc is tied to the cases because of his work with Interpol. It won't be pleasant if I am wrong and he is involved. I never take pleasure in uncovering a dirty cop."

"Who says he's dirty?" said Sill.

"Right now, nobody. But if I find a link between him and Mottola, he is dirty."

* * *

After a few more questions, suggestions, and speculations, the lunch meeting broke up.

"Are we still on for tonight?" asked Blaine.

"Pick me up at seven," Sill said with a smile. "Provided you get out of the dungeon by then."

Blaine picked up their checks, walked to the cashier, and paid the bill. Sill came up beside him, put her hand on his, and, giving it a slight squeeze, said, "Thanks." Then, outside, they left in opposite directions.

CHAPTER 23

Back in the dungeon, Blaine resumed his culling through the files. He searched for that one thing he was sure Dutronc missed. He did not question Dutronc's abilities. It is not uncommon for a detective to miss what a fresh pair of eyes might see.

It is not unusual for a serial killer to use the same M.O. Most were creatures of habit. What Blaine found curious was the gun. The serial killers he studied were typical gun owners. They had or had access to multiple weapons. The killer may prefer one type of weapon over another. This was true when the average citizen had limited access to guns. This unsub used the same weapon for each killing. Why? Why not toss it? Why risk being caught with it? He could not get the why out of his head. Blaine found cases where serial killers used the same weapon. However, never spanning years—let alone decades.

He added pictures to his board for the next three hours and filled his legal pad with notes and questions. By the time he added the last photo, he was mentally and physically drained. He had pictures of eight dead people on his murder board. There was Chevalier, Satie, Ughi, Galli, Poulenc, Torres, Almeda. And Anthony Mottola. The same gun murdered all. By the same person?

Blaine studied his board for one last time and then took a break. He knew it was common for answers to nagging questions to appear out of nowhere. He knew he would find the answer after he put the question out of his mind.

Blaine stood with his hands on his hips, studying the faces on the murder board. He looked down at the pile of files, confident the answers were there. But they would not come tonight, and he had to put these eight faces out of his mind. At least for the night.

* * *

Blaine showered and shaved. He put on a new Western shirt. It was dark blue with the repeated design of crossed six-shooters. His snakeskin boots had a sheen and his silver buckle was polished. He admired his reflection in the full-length mirror. He picked up his grey Stetson and set it on his head. *That should do the trick,* he thought to himself. He checked his watch and then headed out the door, turning off the lights.

Across town, Judee Sill was also getting dressed. Butterflies filled her stomach. She liked Hal, and she was sure he liked her. Still, this was their first date. They had met for lunch at least once a week. This was the first time he had asked her out. She chose a long-sleeved Western shirt with different-colored roses. Her favorite flower. Judee pressed her jeans, and she donned her new lizard-skin boots purchased that afternoon. She had a pink cowgirl hat and admired her new look in her full-length mirror. *Look out, cowboy. This cowgirl's got you in her sights!* she thought.

Blaine and Sill had hit it off from the start. They first met at the Mottola crime scene, and both had military experience. Blaine was an M.P. with the Marines, and Sill was a physician with the Navy. Blaine had seen Sill in her unflattering, figure-hiding scrubs and a few figure-obscuring oversized sweatshirts. Dutronc had concluded the two were an item. But were they? She did seem pleased to see him, maybe even a little excited. They never held hands, but Judee found ways to make contact. She would put her hand on his or stand beside him with their bodies brushing one another. He enjoyed these nuances in their relationship, even if he did not know how to respond. To ask her out was a big step for Blaine, who had not been on a date since leaving the army. Tonight, he was back in high school with sweaty palms and a racing heart. *Why?* He thought. *I am a grown man and have been on dates before.* Before he knew it, he was in front of Judee's house. He got out of the Camaro, grabbed his hat. He walked with confidence to her door.

Judee was still admiring her appearance when she heard the yellow bird pull upfront. She hurried to the door and arrived just as her date knocked. Not wanting to appear over-anxious, she had stopped and counted to ten. Then, with deliberate steps, she reached the door and opened it. She willed herself to keep herself calm. Judee invited Hal in as she gathered her purse and hat. After a moment, she looked around and announced she was ready.

Hal waited as Judee locked her door and walked her to the Camaro. *He's the perfect gentleman,* Judee thought to herself. Her heart pounded in her ears, and she was positive Hal could hear it as he walked beside her. Neither was aware of the nervous tension between them.

Judee hadn't been on a date in three years. Not since before she moved to Mexia. Her work kept her busy, and no one at work attracted her attention. Most were married, and the others were much younger. The last thing she wanted was to be teased about robbing someone's cradle. Never the club-hopper, Judee didn't visit those places where she might meet someone.

Before leaving the service, for a short time, Hal dated Carmen, a fellow M.P. He thought they were getting serious when, without warning, she broke it off. Hal discovered she had also been dating Hal's best friend, and she said yes when his friend popped the question. He was new to the Sheriff's Office when he met Judee. The murder of A.C. and other mundane assignments kept him busier than he thought he would be. Especially in a small community like Mexia.

Their first stop was Pete's in Waco for ribs. Nerves kept the conversation to a minimum during the ride to the eatery.

Neither wanted to talk about work, and finding a topic of interest proved difficult. However, things loosened up with ribs, a baked potato, and a beer. Hal liked Judee's laugh, and his smile captivated her.

The conversation continued on the ride to The Oaks, a dance hall just west of Waco. Once inside, they found a table, ordered another beer, and watched the action.

"Shall we?" Hal stood with his hand outreached.

"Thought you would never ask." Judee smiled.

The two would dance several times before taking a break. They danced with ease the Texas Two-Step and had fun with the line dances. In addition, they enjoyed the occasional slow dance. No one would have guessed that the couple was on their first date.

Almost midnight, the Camaro pulled up to Judee's house. The conversation was more animated on the way home. Each complimented the other on their prowess on the dance floor. The nervousness ever so present at the start of the evening was gone.

Hal jumped out and opened the passenger door for his date. They walked hand in hand. Hal stood as Judee retrieved her key and waited until she unlocked the door. He squeezed her hand and said, "Good night. Let's do this again."

"Let's." She stood there like a high-school girl. Unsure of what she should say or do. After an awkward pause, she smiled and stepped into the house.

Judee gazed at Hal as he turned and walked back to the Camaro.

Judee said, "Wait." She hastened to him. "There is something I have wanted to say all night." She reached up and gave him a gentle kiss on the lips. Before she could turn and go, Hal drew her into him and returned the kiss. However, his was a more deliberate gesture.

They stood in silence, Judee in Hal's embrace. "Whew," she said. "I am glad I got that off my chest."

"Yes, ma'am," said Hal. "Yes. I am sure glad we had that conversation."

Judee laughed, gave him a quick kiss on the cheek. Before Hal could react, Judee was out and running to her door. In a second, the door was closed. Judee leaned against it as if to prevent an intruder from entering. She was smiling and hugging herself. She couldn't see the blush she was feeling.

Hal drove home with a smile on his face. He tapped the song *My Girl* on the wheel.

Both pleased with the evening's outcome, each resisted the temptation to call and continue the evening's magic.

* * *

Everyone noticed a change in Blaine's demeanor in the office early Monday morning. He had a smile on his face and a new bounce in his step. Some, especially the women, looked at each other, grinned, and nodded a knowing nod.

Sheriff Hazelwood followed his deputy to the break room. The sheriff watched until Blaine had fixed his coffee, then said, "I am assuming things went well on Saturday."

Hal looked up, smiled, and shrugged. "I do not know what you are talking about."

"Yeah. Right. But I am not the only one noticing a change in you this morning."

Blaine shrugged and then returned to the files. After the sheriff left, he leaned back in his chair. Eyes closed; he relived the night. He picked up the phone to call, but decided against it. Instead, he put the receiver down and began reading his notes from his time in the dungeon.

CHAPTER 24

"Boss, it's time we met."

"When and where?"

"How about two? Down in the dungeon."

"Great, Hal. I'll call Charlie and see if he and Sill can meet with us."

Blaine hung up the phone and examined his murder board.

* * *

Blaine and Hazelwood were in the dungeon, reviewing the murder board, when they heard the elevator doors open. Chief Musselwhite was by himself.

"Where is Sill?" asked the sheriff.

"It's just the three of us."

"Why?"

"Got a call." It was Musselwhite coming down the hall. "Cindy Walker, ninety-nine, passed in her sleep. Her grandson found her this morning when he checked on her. Nothing unusual or suspicious. A routine call, but it makes her unavailable for this confab."

Turning to his deputy, Hazelwood said, "OK, Blaine, this is your meeting."

###

Hazelwood and Musselwhite sat at the table facing the murder board. The files were in a stack between them. Blaine wanted each to review the files as he explained his theory.

The deputy sheriff took his two colleagues through his notes and the individual files. He was methodical as he did so. He began with the Auguste Chevalier murder in Paris. Blaine agreed with Dutronc. It was the first murder, even though it was years before the others.

"What makes you tie his murder to the others?" asked Musselwhite.

"The M.O. As with all the others, they shot him first in the chest and then between the eyes."

"And this is consistent with all the others?" Hazelwood asked.

"All the murders are identical except for Chevalier and Mottola."

Everyone looked at the Chevalier file. Musselwhite asked, "What makes those two different?"

"Starting with Chevalier and ending with our murder, they shot each in the chest and then in the head. Chevalier is different because there was a note stuffed in his mouth. And, of course, they burned A.C."

"Yes, but they dumped Satie and Ughi in the river," Hazelwood pointed out.

"Each of the murders is unique. After a lengthy hiatus between Chevalier and these two, Inspector Dutronc of Interpol believes it was a feeble attempt to prevent or delay the discovery of the bodies."

"They burned A.C. Doesn't that follow the Satie-Ughi deal?"

"Doesn't feel like that, chief. A.C. often is out of town, and it may have been days or weeks before someone discovered the body."

"So?" asked the sheriff.

"Our murder seems to have another element to it. Whoever this unsub is, they needed to desecrate the body. Just killing the man was not enough. When we find –"

"You mean If," inserted the chief.

"When," continued Blaine, "we find him, then we'll have the answers."

His audience asked a few more questions but let him run through his presentation without interruption. Then Blaine detailed what they knew of the murders of Sergio Galli, Jean Poulenc, Andres Torres, and Daniel Almeda.

"You appear to be spending a lot of time on these European murders."

"I can't argue with that," said Blaine.

"But not so much on our murder."

"Chief, I understand your concern. But the answer to who murdered Mottola is on this murder board. I haven't found it yet. But, trust me, it is there."

The chief persisted, "But, how can you be so sure.?"

"Three things. First, a single factor—the bullet connects all the murders. They murdered each in the same manner. Ballistics say they murdered each with the same gun."

"Are you sure?" It was Sheriff Hazelwood's turn to raise doubts. "How strong is the evidence they used the same gun?"

Blaine grabbed his legal pad and flipped pages and said, "Standard ballistics," and handed a series of photographs of bullets. "As you can see, all striations show they used the same weapon. A twenty-five-caliber pistol." Blaine looked up and said, "This report is from Interpol. The Paris police drew the same conclusions when comparing the bullets recovered from the French shootings." He let this information sink in. Then added, "I sent them photos of the Mottola bullets, and Interpol confirmed the bullets came from the same weapon."

"But does that mean this unsub pulled the trigger for each murder?"

"There is an unknown subject. But I am convinced we are very close to giving that unsub a name. As for being the only trigger man, Interpol and the French consider it likely to be the same perpetrator."

Sheriff Hazelwood said, "OK, we have the same weapon,

and the same person may or may not have fired it. What else convinces you you're on the right track?" He was pointing to the pictures on the murder board.

"Ross Bagdesarian. He is the common link between every murder, including the one in Mexia."

"But he doesn't come on the scene until years after Chevalier, right?"

"Depends," said Blaine, hedging his bets.

"On what?" persisted the chief.

"On whether the youth in the note is Bagdesarian. Interpol and the Paris police believe the youth in the note is Bagdesarian. His mother was Scottish and his father Russian."

"You gotta be kidding," said Musselwhite. "Really? The youth is Bagdesarian?"

"Yes. There was a nasty divorce, and his mother had full custody. Then, when Bagdesarian was a young teen, thirteen or fourteen, they murdered his mother in front of him."

"Wow!" said the sheriff. "What a way to begin the most difficult period in a young man's life."

"It gets worse."

"Worse than witnessing the murder of your mother?"

"Hard as it seems, yes." Blaine waited a beat before continuing. "His father kidnapped him. A member of the Russian Mafia, he was a strict authoritarian. At some point, the old man had a stroke. That's when Bagdesarian made his escape."

"And Chevalier?"

"The working theory today is Chevalier was the hitman hired by the father to murder Bagdesarian's mother. It is unfortunate, but growing up in Russia with an authoritarian parent meant the kid missed out on the freedoms and experiences his peers celebrated."

"So, Bagdesarian is our primary suspect?" asked the chief.

"No." Blaine turned his back on his colleagues and studied the board himself. "His name comes up with every murder.

Even that of A.C., but we can't place him in the vicinity."

"Was he in the States when they murdered Mottola?"

Turning again to face his colleagues, Blaine said, "Still trying to confirm. We know Bergman was in contact with him, but we cannot place Bagdesarian in the country. Let alone Texas, at the time of the fire."

After a pause, Musselwhite asked, "Why do you assume the key to solving the Mottola murder is on that board?"

"We have hit a brick wall. Limiting our search to Texas has produced no suspects."

"But we do have suspects," said Blaine, handing each a sheet with names. He took a seat opposite them. "The unsub is at the top of the list. This is because there is a possibility, he is not one of those listed."

There was a collective "Huh?" from Musselwhite and Hazelwood.

"Let's assume Interpol Inspector Dutronc is correct," and Blaine paused. "That A.C.'s death is somehow linked to these unsolved murders in Europe."

"Go on," encouraged the sheriff.

Clearing his throat, Blaine continued "Then we may not have a complete picture."

"So," said Musselwhite, "This Dutronc fellow is holding back."

"I don't know," Blaine said shrugging his shoulders." Anything is possible."

"Okay, Hal," said Hazelwood. "Forget what you don't know, based on what you do know, who tops the list?"

"Ross Bagdesarian," said Blaine, "is my primary suspect. This doesn't mean he pulled the trigger, but he may have orchestrated the murders. We can link Bagdesarian with every murder on the board."

"Who is Lucio Dalla?" asked Hazelwood. "I don't remember his name being mentioned with any of the murders."

"He could be our unsub at the top of the list."

"How?" asked the sheriff.

As he looked at his colleagues, Blaine explained Dalla was Bagdesarian's muscle man. "No one has called him by name. Bergman said Dalla is the quiet type. However, Bergman believes Dalla to be a cold-blooded killer."

"So," Hazelwood began, "he could be our silent killer. Working in the shadows."

"That's one theory," Blaine agreed.

"But wouldn't his name come up somewhere?" asked Musselwhite.

"From what I have been able to determine," said Blaine. "Dalla is present. He is there but not a participant in any meeting or dealing anyone has with Bagdesarian. He is nearby, observing."

"What about Bergman?" asked Hazelwood.

"He is a known associate of Bagdesarian's. Therefore, he gets included by association only. At least, at this point. That could change as I get more information from my European sources.

"I see you have included Dutronc. Still consider him a dirty cop?" asked Hazelwood.

"I hate to consider that. But except for Chevalier and Mottola, his name comes up with every other murder.

"For Pete's sake, Blaine, he is the lead investigator," said Musselwhite with exasperation.

"Maybe," Blaine said without conviction. "I still must keep my options open. He wouldn't be the first cop going rogue. So I'll consider him only as a last resort, OK?"

"As a last resort!" said Musselwhite.

"You have left someone off," said Hazelwood.

"Ragsdale?" asked Blaine, anticipating where the sheriff was heading.

"I don't think he has been honest, and I am confident he knows more than he has shared with us," said Hazelwood.

"I agree," said Musselwhite.

"You both are right. It is clear Ragsdale knows more than he's letting on. However, I do not consider him a suspect." Blaine waited for a comment, then added, "Where is the motive?"

Everyone was quiet for a minute.

"Look, I need more information before bringing Ragsdale back for questioning. I do not believe he had anything to do with our murder. Nor do I believe he is involved with any other murders on the board," Blaine protested.

"So," Sheriff Hazelwood spoke up, "Why bring him in?"

"He may let us tighten our focus on one or two of those on the board or give us a new suspect."

"Think he knows who murdered his friend?"

"I don't think he knows for sure. However, he may have an idea. I need to convince him to share his suspicions."

Hazelwood asked, "When?"

"When?" repeated Blaine.

"When are you bringing him back in?"

"Soon," said Blaine. "Soon."

"I want to be there," said Hazelwood.

"Copy that." Blaine gathered his notes, looked at the board, and the meeting was over.

Two DAYS AFTER the meeting in the dungeon, Blaine called Harold Ragsdale back to the sheriff's station for another conversation. As Hal walked in through the back entrance the dispatcher said, "You have a visitor."

"Who is it?" The dispatcher checked the log, "A Harold Ragsdale."

"Great. Where is he?"

The dispatcher smiled and said, "In the lobby. He said you were expecting him."

"Thanks," Hal said and offered the dispatcher a two-fingered salute.

Blaine stopped at his boss's office. The sheriff was on the phone, so Blaine mouthed, "He's here."

Hazelwood put his hand over the phone and in a soft voice asked, "Your office?"

Blaine gave a thumbs up and was gone. Five minutes later, the three men were at the conference table in Blaine's office. He and the sheriff were on one side and Ragsdale on the opposite. The meeting was friendly. Everyone chatted for a few minutes before getting down to business.

Blaine picked seven pictures of the murder victims out of his file. "Mr. Ragsdale."

"Harold is fine."

"Mr. Ragsdale," Blaine continued, wanting to keep the business portion of the meeting formal. "We have hit a brick wall with your friend's murder investigation, and we could use your help."

"I was wondering how it was going. How may I help?"

"I believe the key to solving Mr. Mottola's murder may be in solving several murders in Europe—France, Italy, Spain, and Portugal."

"Wow. How did Anthony's murder become international?" asked Ragsdale.

"There are a series of murders occurring over several decades."

"May I ask how many?"

"Seven, including Mr. Mottola. In previous discussions, you mentioned you and Mr. Mottola did some clandestine work. I am assuming this was outside the States?"

"Yes. Our primary field of operation was the Middle East. However, we would sometimes find ourselves in South America, and yes, in Europe," said Ragsdale.

"I am going to show you six faces. They were murdered in the same manner as A.C. Let me know if you recognize any of them." Blaine laid the pictures down, naming them as he did so. "Alfred Satie, Jean Poulenc, Bruno Ughi, Sergio Galli, Andres Torres, and Daniel Almeda."

Ragsdale picked up and examined each photograph. Then he set one photo aside. "This one—can't remember his name."

"Bruno Ughi," said Blaine.

"If you say so. A.C. and I knew him as Prince."

"Prince? Was he royalty?"

"Nah," said Ragsdale with a chuckle. "He always had a copy of *The Prince* by Machiavelli. He enjoyed quoting from the book. Said he was some distant relative of the family." Ragsdale picked up the photo again. "We think it made him feel superior to quote from the book, but..." In the end, Ragsdale let the sentence hang before asking, "How did he get his due?"

"They shot him and Sergio Galli."

"Two shots, like Anthony?"

"Good guess," said Blaine. "And then tied together and

dumped in the Arno River. Across from the Pitti Palace."

"Ironic, isn't it?" said Ragsdale. "Pretending to be related to Machiavelli, only to be executed and dumped in front of Machiavelli's palace."

Sheriff Hazelwood spoke for the first time. "Pretend? Do you mean he wasn't? Or is it you just didn't believe him?"

"He was not the brightest candle on any cake," said Ragsdale. "Nobody considered him believable. Too many of his stories were false. We doubted his quotes from the book."

"You sure?" asked Hazelwood.

"Positive. When some stories proved less than accurate, we did some checking. For example, we found over half the quotes Prince attributed to Machiavelli—"

"Were not in the book," said Blaine. "Bingo!"

"What about the others?" asked Hazelwood.

"None of them look familiar, and I don't recognize the names." Ragsdale put the photo back on the table. "Any suspects?"

"Suspects? No," deadpanned Blaine. "We do have some persons of interest." With that, Blaine laid three new photos on the table. He named them as he set them down. "Alan Bergman, Lucio Dalla, Ross Bagdesarian."

Ragsdale let out a laugh. "You have got to be kidding."

"You don't think they are capable?" asked Blaine.

"Only one is capable," and touched the picture of Dalla. "This one is a ruthless killer. He is more than capable of murder."

"But not our killer?" said Hazelwood.

"Dalla likes it up close and personal. He would stab you, garrote you, or put a plastic bag over your head. He carries a gun, but my guess is that's for show and intimidation. As far as we know, none of his victims were shot. My guess is he hated sudden loud noises. Nope. He is not your man."

"And the other two?" asked the sheriff.

"I have met Bergman. As far as I am concerned, he little more than a con man. I suspect the only way he can tell the truth is by accident." Ragsdale looked at the two across the table. "My impression is he could not kill a mosquito on his arm. Even if it is about to inject malaria into the man's blood."

"And Bagdesarian?" asked Blaine.

"Too pretty!" said Ragsdale. "I heard he had a rough life growing up. Now he wants nothing to do with the bad stuff."

"The bad stuff?" asked Hazelwood.

"You know. Bagdesarian doesn't mind ordering someone to be beaten up or killed. He just doesn't want to be there. He doesn't want to watch, let alone do the deed." Ragsdale watched the two and waited. "Tell me about the killings. The weapon or anything else unique."

"In each case, the weapon is a twenty-five-caliber handgun," said Blaine. "Easy to conceal, not much noise, and lethal up close."

"Ballistics confirm they used the same gun each time," said Hazelwood.

"He, or she, is a pro."

"Could it be a woman?" asked Hazelwood.

"My experience is women prefer poison. But a twenty-five-caliber is lightweight and concealed with ease. Whoever is doing the killing likes the weapon's feel and is not likely to change," said Ragsdale.

"That's what we considered. Those," Blaine added pointing at the last three photos, "are the only ones connected to multiple victims."

"Sheriff, you are missing something. Someone else can tie everything together for you."

With hesitation, Blaine asked, "Ever hear of Jacques Dutronc?"

"Can't say that I have. Why?"

"Dutronc is an Interpol inspector and is head of a mafia task force. He has investigated all the ones I showed you."

"There is more?" asked Ragsdale.

"Oh, it is my experience. There is always more," said

Hazelwood.

"The first known murder with this unique M.O. was Auguste Chevalier in Paris. Murdered in the early eighties."

"Your Interpol guy involved?"

Both Hazelwood and Blaine shook their heads. "Not that we have been able to discern."

"A part of Anthony's case?" asked Ragsdale.

"No reason to be part of the investigation."

"Maybe so. Listen, the person you are looking for will have ties to all the murders. Including the first and the last."

"Anything else you care to share?" asked Blaine.

"Keep looking. You'll find your answers. I don't know that I would rule out your Interpol guy. But don't get excited and pin your hopes on him. Not likely to be him."

"You said a hacker identified you and A.C.," said Blaine.

"Yes. Someone well connected, from what we could learn."

"Military? Intelligence? Law?" suggested Blaine.

"All the above, and none of the above," said Ragsdale. "I would find it hard to believe someone in the intelligence community, regardless of affiliation, would be responsible."

"Why is that?" asked Hazelwood.

"Simple. We may not like each other, but we respect each other. We know the havoc and danger it causes when a leak occurs." Ragsdale took a breath. "Look, let's say someone leaks CIA information. It might prove deadly for the CIA, but it causes concern for everyone else. No one wants that headache. Trust me, it is not an intelligence leak."

"So, someone in the law enforcement community or the military establishment?"

"Good guess, sheriff, but don't forget academia. Anyone who has been burned by the establishment could be our man."

Blaine asked, "Hasn't Interpol looked at all this?"

"At this point, I don't know and don't care. Listen, Blaine, I understand you were an M.P."

"True." The deputy nodded affirmatively.

"And you investigated crimes before. Theft, assault, murder. Right?"

"All the above," assured Blaine.

Hazelwood reminded him, "Then you understand the key to solving any crime. You must proceed as if no one has thought of your line of investigation. You need to watch your six. Your pro may monitor your actions to ensure you are not getting too close. They won't hesitate to take you down if you become a threat."

After Ragsdale was gone, Blaine and Hazelwood sat opposite each other. "What do you think?" asked the sheriff.

"We have more than we had."

"Yes, but did it help?"

"Not sure." Blaine studied his notes from the meeting. "I just don't know."

There was a long pause, and the sheriff stood. "You know Ragsdale has more secrets." Blaine did not respond but shrugged his shoulders in a questioning manner. The sheriff watched his deputy for a moment and then left.

Blaine sat staring at the murder board. He laced his fingers behind his head and closed his eyes. A moment later, he opened them, slapped the table with his palms, and stood up. "I'm coming after you," and walked out of the dungeon.

CHAPTER 26

Hal's plane touched down at 9:49 am. It arrived at gate 33 at 10:16. Hal was one of the last passengers to deplane, and Judee feared he had missed his flight. Then she saw him come through the doors to the baggage claim carousel. She rushed toward him. They embraced and shared an extended kiss.

"Welcome to Miami. How was your flight? Are you hungry? Do you see your baggage?"

"Slow down, little lady. Give me a chance to catch my breath. Now, the flight was fine. I am always hungry, and yes, that black thing over there," pointing to the carousel, "is mine."

Judee blushed at her gushiness and then settled down. "Your room is at the Marriott."

"Close to yours?" he said with a laugh.

"Not even close. I am staying with my sister. Mom and dad are next to yours, so have at it if you want to do some recon." Hal took a thoughtful pose. "Just a warning. They are doing some recon on their own."

"So, what is on the agenda?"

"Not much. You are on your own, so don't get drunk and hit the gentlemen's clubs."

"Can't hit those joints."

"Oh?"

"I have been called many things, but never a gentleman."

Judee laughed, "Yes, you are more than a little rough around the edges," and she kissed him.

"You'll come to the church with my parents around 4:30. It will be boring as we take a few more pictures and go through the rehearsal part. Rehearsal dinner is at Donegan's, sis's favorite seafood restaurant."

"And tonight?" Hal wondered.

"Party time. You with the groom and his friends. I'm in charge of my sis's party."

"Do I need to worry?"

"If you mean what I think you mean, you can relax. Unlike the two of us, these are God-fearing people who live boring lives."

"How boring?"

"Sis is an elementary teacher, and Rob, her husband-to-be, is a banker at Credence Bank."

"Strait-laced?" asked Hal.

"Starched straight," and both laughed.

*   *   *

Hal fitted in with Rob and his friends, all military vets representing every branch of the service. The guys spent the evening telling war stories and playing poker. Hal presumed they rigged the game to favor the guest of honor. But, alas, Rob was a master at the game and cleaned up with no one's help.

It was a simple and elegant wedding. Hal knew most of the audience had their eyes on the bride, but had a hard time ignoring his girlfriend. Her gown was a strapless, floor-length teal that highlighted Judee's eyes. He was in heaven as he held her in his arms and danced the night away.

Much to his chagrin, Judee sent him back to the hotel with her parents. Judee agreed to stay behind and help clean up the reception hall and take care of things for her sister. She saw Hal off at 11:30 the following day and spent the rest of the day cleaning up the house and looking after her sister's German shepherd. There was no space at the boarding center for the dog until Sunday afternoon. She would take the last flight out that evening.

"Well, your guy seems all right," said her father.

Her mother elbowed him. "What he means is Hal seems to care for you a lot."

"And what she means," said her father, pointing to her mother, "When can we expect a repeat performance?"

"I am not asking when she and Hal are getting married," her mother's voice was authoritative.

"Could have fooled me," her father said, trying to stifle a laugh. "Ever since you knew he would be here, you kept wondering if they were serious and when he would pop the question."

Unable to contain her joy, Judee said, "We are still in the friend stage."

"Uh-hum," said her father under his breath.

"We have not discussed a future together."

"Your body language betrays you. Neither of you may have spoken the words, but the thoughts are there."

Judee changed the subject, and the conversation went in many directions. Each time, the conversation wound up back with Hal and Judee.

Her mother took Judee's hands and, in a severe tone, asked, "Do you love him?"

"Gee, Mom," Judee said, looking at the floor. "No one has ever uttered the L-word."

"Fair enough," her mother said. "Then let me ask you this. Could you love him?"

"Yes." It was a soft whisper.

"Do I need to give him a kick in the pants to get to ball rolling?" her father asked.

"Gee, Dad. No!"

* * *

Hal was waiting for Judee at the luggage carousel. He picked up her bags and escorted her to the Camaro. They drove to her house in silence. They both had a lot to take in.

Parking in front of her house, he turned and asked, "Well, did I pass?"

"I do not know what you mean?" Judee said, looking over her eyebrows.

"Oh, yeah? No one has interrogated more thoroughly," Hal said with a broad smile.

"By whom?"

"Your parents, for starters, especially your mother."

"Not Dad?"

"Nah," said Hal. "He asked the usual. Your mother was the devious one, asking some rather provocative and personal questions."

"My parents are protective. What can I say?"

"Then there was Rob, his best man, and the three others at the poker game."

"Did you win?"

"Of course not. It wasn't my night. It was Rob's."

"So, you let him win?" asked Judee.

"Not on your life. Let's put it this way. When Hoyle invented the game, he had Rob in mind. Your new brother-in-law is a whiz at it. He needed no help from us. Being the big winner of the night."

"What did you think of my family?"

With a huge smile, Hal said, "They are great. Your sister has married a good man. Not as good as me, but he'll do in a pinch." Judee slapped Hal's arm.

"I have to admit Rob has been perfect for Sis."

Hal said, "You have the day off tomorrow, but I don't, and need to get some rest. Big day tomorrow."

"I am pooped. I'm glad I took the extra day." Judee held her hand over a yawn.

"Oh, tell your dad to put the shotgun away."

"Shotgun?"

"When it is time, I will do it upright."

"So, you love me?" Judee said with excitement.

"I didn't say that." Hal leaned over and put her arms around her.

Judee had a hurt look on her face.

Taking her chin and pointing her head toward him, he said, "I did not deny it, either." He kissed her. "Now, let's get you into your house before the neighbors call the cops."

"But you are the cops."

"No, ma'am, I am not. Cops are city folk. I am a Limestone County deputy sheriff. And I deserve a little respect."

She bent across and gave him one last kiss and opened the car door before he could get around the Camaro. Hal carried her luggage to the front door and waited for her to unlock and open it.

She turned and started to say something., but Hal got there first. "Proud to be of service to you, young woman. Now, you have a good evening." He kissed her forehead, turned, and Judee watched as the Camaro pulled out of sight.

CHAPTER 27

Chief Musselwhite and Sheriff Hazelwood were late for the meeting. Fire Marshall Anita Kerr, nicknamed AK47, was leading the proceedings. Medical Examiner Judee Sill and Deputy Sherriff Hal Blaine were on either side. Chief Musselwhite sat next to the medical examiner while Sheriff Hazelwood sat next to his deputy.

The fire marshal stood and opened the meeting. "After the fire at Triple M, I put everything collected into evidence bags, sealed, and initialed. I put those bags and notes and photos into this box." AK held up a banker's box with *TRIPLE M FIRE* written on one end.

"I followed protocol. But then my father had a stroke. Taking care of him put me out of the office for an extended period." AK looked around the table for confirmation, objections, or questions. There were none.

"When I returned to work, Deputy Blaine and I went through the box. We found five small evidence bags not yet processed."

Blaine said, "We sent them to the crime lab for processing." He paused and added, "The box remained in the active case room. The chain of custody is intact."

"OK," said Musselwhite. "OK. We can establish the chain of custody. What did you find?"

AK began. "Three of the bags led us nowhere." She held up the first bag. "This bag had a non-descript button. Most likely snagged by a ruff edge and popped off. It is like buttons found on the victim's shirts; one shirt was missing a button." Next, she held up a second bag. "We found a small piece of paper with some writing. It matches a page from a journal we found in A.C.'s house."

"And the journal page?"

"Just some random notes. It is possible he was looking for something to add to his inventory. Nothing I would consider a motive for murder. Then the piece of paper recovered had fold marks. The way he folded the page suggests he used it as a bookmark. It wasn't in a book, so it's only a guess. Again, nothing on the paper or in the journal suggests the writing was of any significance."

"Any idea how that piece of paper or any of this stuff remained unscathed by the fire and water?"

"Fires are living, breathing things. Just like fingerprints, no two are identical. Sometimes, the entire contents of the building are gone. Other times, like this one, there may be part of the building ignored by the fire. I found these items in a corner furthest from the fire. That's all I can tell you."

"OK. What about number three?" asked Hazelwood.

"It contained some fibers from a wool coat. Not domestic, but with online shopping and every store selling coats from every part of the world..." AK let the statement die. Then she said, "I doubt it will take us very far."

"That leaves two bags. Let's hope they are more productive," said the chief.

AK gave a nod and smile to the chief. "Each bag contained a cigarette butt. One is a domestic brand, Marlboro, and the second is a cigarette that had brown cigarette paper and was a popular French brand."

"And the importance?" asked the sherriff.

"We got lucky," said AK.

"Very lucky," added Blaine.

"We pulled usable DNA from each."

"Have you been able to identify the smoker?"

"Not yet. We have compared what we found with all available domestic databases. This is time-consuming; the results will take some time."

"How much time, AK?" Hazelwood asked.

"If they are in a database, we should be able to identify them within a matter of weeks."

"What about those databases which you can't access?"

AK took a seat as Blaine stood up. It was his meeting now. "We want to know the identity of each smoker. We know it is a domestic blend, most likely Marlboro, one of the world's most popular brands." Blaine let the information sink in. "Marlboro is the most popular cigarette brand in France. So, although it is a domestic brand, it doesn't mean a local discarded it."

Hazelwood sat, taking notes. "I'm trying to quit," and laid a pack of Marlboros on the table.

Musselwhite looked at the cigarettes, then at his friend, and then at Blaine. "Are you saying the cigarette belonged to Bart?"

Blaine laughed. "No, not at all. But it shows how popular that brand is."

"Enough about my smokes," said the sheriff. "What about that brown thing?" Hazelwood pointed to the fifth bag.

"This is a Gauloises. The most popular French-made cigarette."

"Anyone sell these in this area?" asked the chief.

"Nope. However, we found an outlet in Dallas and another in Houston. So, as far as we know, that's it. But, of course, a small smokehouse might special-order the brand for a customer," said Blaine. "Back to the subject at hand. If we can find a match to the DNA on these cigarettes, then we may be closer to identifying our killer. But, remember, although the cigarette is French, they are available in Texas. So, we will have to wait and see."

"Dr. Sill, do you have access to foreign databases?"

"No, sheriff. I don't."

"But I do," said Blaine. "A friend of mine, Special Agent Bill Fries with the FBI International Unit is in London. We have kept in touch, and I am hoping if we provide him with a DNA sample, he can run it through the European databases for us."

"Tell me, Hal, do you have a suspect?" asked the chief.

"Charlie, we have a person of interest," said the sheriff. "However, we cannot be too careful. He appears to have eyes and ears around the globe."

"Law enforcement?" asked the chief.

"Yes, but that is all I will say right now." Then Hazelwood stood and explained the problems facing the investigation. And with that, the meeting adjourned.

* * *

After the chief and the sheriff left, the three remained behind. Everyone relaxed and asked about AK's father, and Judee's sister's wedding. In addition, they discussed the burgeoning romance between Hal and Judee.

"OK, here is where we are," said Blaine. "As much as I hate to admit it, our primary suspect is an Interpol investigator: Jacques Dutronc. Judee and I met with him when they were at a conference in San Antonio." Judee avoided making eye contact with Hal. "And I have talked with him by phone."

"More than once?" asked AK.

"Yes. At least two times," said Hal.

Judee was silent for a long time. "I still don't see how he has gone from colleague to suspect."

"We need to first remember Interpol is not law enforcement. They cannot make any arrest on their own. Nor can they compel any local agency to make an arrest at their behest."

"Then what do they do, and how is that relevant?" asked a confused Sill.

"We are a small community. Most of what we know about Interpol is based on what we see on television, in the movies, or read in books. And that information is not always accurate." Blaine looked at the others for understanding. "Bill Fries often works with them. From what he has told me, I learned they are a consulting and training agency. They can steer investigations in a particular direction. They communicate through a secure network. No reason exists for an investigator assigned to the Paris office to be in Italy. Or anywhere else. So why is our friend Jacques involved in all these cases?"

"Is it forbidden?" asked AK.

"I talked with the U.S. Interpol office in New York," said Blaine. "As you might guess, they were hesitant to talk to me. Especially since I am asking about one of their own. Like us, they are very protective of their own. However, I got them to admit while it was not routine, Jacques' involvement would not have been impossible."

"Look at our case," Blaine went on. Dutronc is the one who told us about the European murders. He connected those murders in Europe to our murder. So he is the common link."

"Not Chevalier," said Sill.

"What?"

"He's not connected with Chevalier. The first murder with this M.O."

"You are right. We can't link Dutronc to the first murder. However, it doesn't mean the link isn't there."

"Or the last," added Sill. "There is nothing to tie him to our little murder."

"That is true, but we have eliminated everything else. And there is the adage, 'Take everything else away, and whatever remains, however illogical...'"

"Is the truth," finished Sill.

"Judee, I know you like this guy. Hey, I like him too. But there are too many coincidences to not at least consider him," Blaine said.

AK added, "And we don't believe in coincidences."

There was an awkward silence when Judee asked, "When

will you send the DNA samples to your friend?"

"Already done."

"When will results be available?"

"Soon, I hope. Fries said he would call when he had something."

Everyone was quiet for a long while.

"Well, I've got to go. I need to check on Dad." AK left, leaving Judee and Hal.

"This has been a lot to take in," Judee said.

"Agreed."

"I think I'll head home."

"Call you later?" Blaine asked.

"No. Not tonight, I need to be alone." Judee did not look at Blaine when she left.

Blaine was left by himself in the conference room. He put the evidence back in the box and took it to the evidence room. As he passed his boss's office, the sheriff waved him in. "Have a seat." Hal did what he was told. "I have read your reports. You are building a strong circumstantial case, but you still need a motive."

"I've been thinking about that," said Blaine.

"Well?" the sheriff asked, encouraging his deputy to talk.

"I keep going back to something Ragsdale said. Way back at the start."

"What did he say?"

"Remember, he said a hacker leaked their identities, locations, and missions."

"Yes."

"Ragsdale also said A.C. saw something that spooked him."

"Yes. Bergman, Bagdesarian and Dalla."

"Yes," Blaine said. "But we have eliminated them. So, what if Dutronc is the hacker? And what if Dutronc is who he saw? Remember, Ragsdale said they had a picture, but not a name."

The sheriff contradicted his deputy. "I thought they had a name, but not a picture."

"Works the same way. What if it was hearing the name or seeing the face that spooked him?"

"And Dutronc recognized A.C.?"

"Right," said Blaine.

"So, Dutronc ties up loose ends by killing A.C. and then attempted to destroy any evidence with the fire." The sheriff had the hint of a smile. "Pretty clever."

"And he almost got away with it."

Hazelwood reminded Blaine, "We still don't have him."

"Maybe. But he is in my crosshairs." Blaine got up to leave. Then, at the door, he said, "I'm outta here."

CHAPTER 28

BACK IN HIS office, Blaine calculated the time difference between London and Mexia and determined his FBI friend might still be in the office. He made the call. Five minutes later, Fries came on the line.

"Special Agent William Fries." The tone was both business-like and friendly.

"Hey. Bill," Blaine said.

"Hal?" said a surprised FBI agent. "How are things in Texas?"

"Some ole, same ole. How are things in jolly old London?"

"Still here, but can't say for how long."

"Quitting? You are too young to retire."

"My time to rotate back Stateside is coming up."

"So, you coming home?"

"Can't say for sure. They can extend my time here or send me to another international branch. Or they can bring me home. Won't learn where I am going for sure for another two or three months."

"Great, I got you in the nick of time," Blaine said.

"Why, what's up?"

Blaine took some time to bring Fries up to date with the Mottola case.

"So, you think you got a dirty cop?"

"I'm not sure. I may have DNA needing running through international databases."

"Want to include Interpol personnel?"

"If you can without raising any red flags."

"Not a problem. Databases here include everyone from the Queen of England on down. Let me check out this Dutronc fellow. Once I get the samples, I should get results in forty-eight to seventy-two hours. If I put a rush on it."

"That will be great," responded Blaine.

"I'll let you know as soon as I have the samples for you," finished Fries.

* * *

As soon as Blaine hung up the phone, it rang. "Limestone County Sherriff's Office, Deputy Blaine," he said.

"Didn't look at caller ID, did you?"

"Sorry, AK. I just got off an international call. My brain is not home yet," Blaine admitted, and they both laughed.

"International call? Sounds important."

"I called Bill Fries, my FBI friend stationed in London. We go back a few years and—"

"He will run our DNA," AK said, finishing the sentence.

Blaine ignored the comment and asked, "What's the verdict?"

"Both cigarette butts had usable DNA. That's the good news."

"What's the bad news?" Blaine asked.

"It will take several days to get the results back."

"OK. I can live with that." Blaine then enquired, "Any idea how they wound up unaffected by the fire?"

"I can't say for sure. Remember when I said fires are unique and no two are alike?"

"Sure."

"Luck is also a variable, and she played a big role in our fire."

"How so?" asked Blaine.

"Remember, the gel used to start the fire had a minor explosion at the beginning?"

Hal nodded his head but said nothing.

"My guess is the cigarettes were outside the intended blast area, and the shock wave sent them scattering."

"Were they found together?"

"No, I checked photos and sketches. They found the evidence at the corner of the building furthest from the blast. Each on a different wall." AK was silent for several minutes. "You still there?" she asked.

"Yes. Just thinking."

"Well, that's dangerous." They both laughed. "You know, Hal, there is no way to determine how long the butts had been in the building."

"Yes, but if my hunch is right, it means we have the strongest suspect since the entire investigation began." Blaine ended the call with excitement.

* * *

"Got a sec?" Blaine asked after the sheriff got off the phone.

"Only a sec. County judge wants a sit-down."

"We are making progress in the Triple M fire."

"It's about time." Blaine had his attention.

"You remember the cigarette butts?"

"Yes," said the sheriff. "One was European."

"Well, I just talked with AK. She assures me there is enough DNA to develop a profile. On both cigarettes."

"That is good news. But when do you get the results?"

Blaine recapped the conversation he had just concluded with the fire marshal.

"Well," the sheriff said, "I guess we can wait a week, right?"

"Yeah. I also talked with Bill Fries, my FBI friend in London. He has agreed to run the profile against databases outside of our purview. Including Interpol employees." Blaine was as excited as a kid in a candy store.

"Earth to Blaine," said the sheriff. "Let's get back to reality.

We don't know how long the butts had been in the store. Even if it turns out the DNA is Dutronc's, that is a long way from putting him at the fire."

"Yes, but an idea is coming into focus. Fries is doing a bit of covert background checking on the Frenchman. We need to determine where he was when Chevalier—"

"The first victim," Hazelwood interrupted in confirmation.

"Right. There is no link between the first and last murders. So if I can put him at or near these two murders, I might build a strong circumstantial case."

"Has he said anything about being in the area before the fire?"

"That's just it. Judee and I talked with him at length in San Antonio. He played dumb throughout the conversation. He never admitted being in Texas, visiting Triple M, or meeting A.C."

"You are still far from being able to extradite him. If that is even an option."

"I am no expert on Interpol, so I did some checking. Did you know Interpol has an office in New York?"

"I believe I heard that somewhere. In fact, you told me. Do you know how big?"

"Five officers. And guess who is not one of the lucky five?"

"Your friend, Jacques Dutronc," said Hazelwood.

"The same," confirmed Blaine. "Not only that, but I confirmed Interpol also has no investigative powers unless the host country grants it."

"And does Jacques have any investigative powers?"

"Depends on who is talking. Jacques says yes, but I haven't been able to confirm. Interpol is a liaison between departments. It is a technicality, but he could investigate the charge to share with other departments. However, he has no authority to make an arrest. No Interpol investigator has that authority."

"Anything else? I can spare three minutes before I am to meet the judge. He will understand if I am a minute or two late."

"Bill said there is a rumor about a single name. They have identified Nino as the assassin. Although believed to be Greek, there is no confirmation of that fact."

"Man or woman?"

"Don't know yet. Fries is looking into it under the pretext he may have a lead."

The sheriff was skeptical. "Won't that draw attention to himself?"

"Fries said not all European law enforcement types have their DNA on file. This is especially true with veterans. So Fries wants to draw Dutronc out for a face-to-face. He hopes this will allow him to get some current DNA as a back-up."

"Quick thinking," Hazelwood said as he stood up. "Keep me posted," and he walked out the door.

* * *

Blaine went as far as he could with the Triple M case and turned his attention to other matters. There were files to be completed and a follow-up to the big rig fire from the week before. He was going through the motions without enthusiasm when his phone rang. After AK chided him the last time she called, he checked the caller ID before picking up.

"Hey, kiddo. How's it going?" Blaine was always happy when Judee called. He hadn't talked with her for several days.

"Great," she said with excitement. "Talked with Sis. They had a wonderful honeymoon cruise. Said she is getting carpal tunnel from all the thank-you notes she needs to write. And then she needs to return some duplicate gifts. Remind me to keep my wedding simple."

"Works for me," said Blaine.

"What does?"

"Us getting married at the courthouse. After all, I have some pull there!" and gave Judee a wink.

It took Sill a few minutes before she realized the joke. "Listen, I am not ready to get married."

"Good, neither am I," confirmed Blaine.

"Besides, who said I wanted to marry you?"

"You did."

"When?"

"With that little conversation, you started after our first date."

There was a pause. Hal could feel her blushing over the phone. Then Sill said, "Oh, that conversation."

"Yup."

"OK, why did you call? Are you breaking our date tomorrow night?"

There was a pause, and Sill said, "Well, as a matter of fact…"

"Who's my rival?"

"Sis. She wants me to come down for a few days. We haven't visited since I came to Mexia."

"There was the wedding."

"That was work. This is pleasure. I am leaving tomorrow morning. It will be quick. I'll be back in the office on Monday. Can you survive?"

"I'll manage." They talked for a few more minutes. Hal had planned on heading home early. But, with the change of plans, he stayed a little longer.

CHAPTER 29

Blaine was busy shutting down for the day. He was back in the dungeon, going through the files once more. The deputy felt that the break they needed to crack open and solve the Mottola murder was near. He shared his enthusiasm with the sherriff, who cautioned him to be careful.

"Most mistakes happen when an over-confident cop submits to their enthusiasm. So keep your head on straight and follow the clues."

Blaine put away the last file and was at the door when his phone rang. He turned out the light and closed the door. He flipped the lights back on and hurried to the phone. "Sheriff's Office, Blaine."

"Hal? Bill Fries. I was hoping I could catch you before you left. Time differences, you know."

"Hey, Bill. You just barely caught me. I was about to walk out. What's up?"

"I have good news."

"Great. I could use some good news. But I am waiting for the other shoe to drop. You know, the bad news part."

"Not in this case, old pal. Only got good news. At least, I think it is."

"OK, lay it on me."

"What would you say if we could check Dutronc's DNA without a database search?"

Blaine asked, "How, pray tell, is that?"

"Aristoteles Savalas is an Interpol inspector here in London. He and I have worked together on several cases. And he is friends with our good inspector."

"OK," said Blaine, not sure where this was going.

"Both of them are smokers. It seems Dutronc was in his office smoking while discussing a case. As luck would have it, I called Savalas just as Dutronc left. Good friends or not, Ari has shared some misgivings he has had with how Dutronc handles certain cases. Apparently, Dutronc may have skirted protocol on a case or two. Anyway, I explained the situation and told him about your case. He grabbed one of Dutronc's cigarettes and is developing a DNA profile as we speak."

"Any idea what brand?"

"My guy is a Marlboro man through and through. Dutronc takes the French line seriously. He tolerates Americans when it serves his purposes. However, whenever possible, he will choose French.

"Let me guess. The cigarette paper is brown."

"What else?"

"So, it is Gauloises?"

"Give the man a rubber duckie!" Fries said without disguising his enthusiasm.

"So, when will it be ready?"

"Give me seventy-two hours. At a minimum."

"Great," said Blaine. "The last time we talked, you mentioned a ghost named Nino or something. Find anything new?"

"As far as anyone knows or will say, Nino is a Greek assassin. Besides the name, he is a Casper, though not so friendly. Where this specter calls home is unknown. Can't even say if Nino is a man or a woman, young or old. Or anything else. Dutronc discovered Nino about ten years ago. A few others claim to have encountered examples of Nino's work. Right now, it is all pretty sketchy, and the trail runs cold as soon as anyone discovers Nino's presence."

"Going back to my favorite Interpol inspector, what can you

tell me about his cross-jurisdictional work?"

"Not a whole lot. As you are aware, Interpol has no authority to detain or arrest anyone. They operate in an advisory role. They also do some specialized training. In the end, Nino seems tied to organized crime. This is Dutronc's specialty. Everyone seems to welcome Dutronc's help when Nino is involved."

"Do you know when Dutronc becomes involved? I mean, does he arrive on the scene before or after they discover a murder?"

Fries was quiet, and Blaine could hear pages ruffling. "I'm still checking. I am sure Dutronc was in Florence before they fished Ughi and Galli from the Arno. So as far as I can determine, our friend was in Florence before they dumped the bodies in the river."

"Any others?"

"Hal, this is a path filled with land mines, and there is no map. So we must tread softly, or we will set off an intellectual IED. What would help is if you tied this guy to your murder in Texas."

"How does that help you?" asked Blaine.

"I can't say for Texas, but here in Europe, an indictment loosens lips."

Blaine considered his options. "The problem is, we have no evidence Dutronc has been in the States. Except when my medical examiner and I met him at the Forensics Conference in San Antonio."

"That's odd. He always seems on the move, and I understand he has been across the pond on more than one occasion. So tell me, when was your murder?" asked Fries.

"Late January."

"This year?"

"Yes, why?" Fries piqued Blaine's curiosity.

"Dutronc was in Dallas in January and February. He was teaching a session on secure communication networks."

"You sure?"

"My partner, Dean Miller, was at the same conference. Not the whole time, mind you, but I know for a fact he and Dutronc were there together."

"How can you be so sure?"

"Miller's desk is next to mine. I am looking at a picture of the two with a provocatively dressed blonde."

"Great. That means I can put Dutronc in the area."

"That's a large area, old boy," said Fries.

"Yeah, but now I know what haystack to search."

"When will you have your profile ready?" asked Fries.

"Today or tomorrow. I will send it to you as soon as I have it."

"Great. Keep me posted,"

Blaine hung up the phone and was unsure what the next move should be. He reviewed his notes from the call. The deputy rang his boss. When the phone went unanswered, he looked at the clock. It was almost 5:30, and Blaine assumed his boss was gone for the day. He walked to the murder board and moved Dutronc's photo over to the suspects' column. He stood and studied the board and, under his breath, said, "Gotcha." He shot the picture with a finger gun. Blaine turned, grabbed his hat, and turned the lights out before closing the door.

CHAPTER 30

"You little scoundrel," Sill said in a playful voice. This was difficult for her, since she was not comfortable with the call. She considered Dutronc to be a friend and colleague. He had also moved to the top of the suspect list for the Triple M murder and fire. Sill, with reluctance, agreed to talk with Dutronc.

Before responding, Dutronc gave a puzzled look at his phone. "Excuse me, *mon ami*, I have no idea what you are talking about."

"I had to hear from my best friend in the Tarrant County Medical Office that you were in town."

"Forgive me. It was a quick trip, and I had no opportunity to call you."

"Are you sure?" Sill said with skepticism. "Jennifer."

"Jennifer?" Dutronc interrupted.

"Yes. Jennifer Warnes. The Tarrant County M.E. Stunning blonde, piercing blue eyes and a laugh you can't get out of your head."

Laughing, Dutronc replied, "Yes, I remember Jennifer. She is hard to forget, but I did not remember her name."

Liar, Sill thought. She fought to keep the word inside.

"Jennifer says you have been there several times over the past three years. In fact."

"Have I?" said a defensive Dutronc.

"She said that you were there for a week. In January."

"But my love, I didn't know you then."

Sill felt a sudden chill. She closed her eyes, took a breath, and said, "So. You were there in January."

"OK. Let's take a step back, as you Texans are fond of saying. What is going on?"

"In San Antonio, you told Deputy Blaine and me that the conference was your first trip to Texas."

"What can I say? Your charm and beauty distracted me," he said. "I apologize. No big thing, right?"

"Was it? Listen, Inspector Dutronc."

"Jacques," he said, trying to soften the situation.

"Inspector Dutronc. I am not accustomed to being lied to and used. Especially by a colleague pretending to be a friend."

"*Je suis désolé*. I am sorry in French, English, and any other language you desire. You are…" he searched quickly for the right word, "amazing."

"Don't try flattery. You do not know what I am capable of."

"Oh, but I do, Dr. Sill, and I admire your work. Now, if you will let me finish, I was saying you are an amazing medical examiner."

"Thank you, but that bridge is burning."

"I understand," said a contrite Dutronc. "We are still friends, at least. Right?"

"Well, we aren't enemies. For the time being, however, I think we best keep it professional."

"I can manage some free time tomorrow. Can we get together?"

"I won't promise anything. What time?"

"Noontime. May I buy you lunch? I owe you that much. I abhor the idea that a Frenchman, especially this Frenchman, might have offended you."

"Call me when you get into town. Like I said, I won't promise, but I will try to make time for you."

"Fair enough. Until tomorrow," said Dutronc and hung up.

Sill frowned at her phone. *What have I gotten myself into?* she thought.

* * *

After talking with Dutronc, Sill called Blaine. "Alright, hot shot. Your hunch was right on the money. He admitted to being in Texas at the time of the Triple M fire."

"How did you get him to come clean?"

"Used Jennifer Warnes' name. She's the medical examiner in Tarrant County. I used a little subterfuge. I said Jenny told me he was there in January."

"Did she?"

Judee laughed. "Nah, Jennifer is a good friend, and we talked about what I needed. I did not want Dutronc calling to confirm and catch me in my own lie. Besides, Jenny has been off for two weeks with a broken leg. Crashed her Harley a few weeks ago."

"And Dutronc never questioned it?" asked Blaine.

"No."

"That doesn't mean he won't attempt to call your friend to confirm," Blaine warned.

"True," said Judee. "That's why I called Jenny before calling the two-faced Frenchman."

"Now what?" asked Blaine.

"To make amends, Dutronc wants to have lunch tomorrow. I've agreed to meet.

him at Delaware Subs. They don't use foam cups except for coffee. All other beverages are in plastic bottles."

"What if he orders coffee?"

"He won't. He prefers water. He said his doctor told him to reduce his caffeine. He said he limits coffee to breakfast and doesn't like soft drinks. So he drinks water with his meals. I can take his bottle under the pretense of personal recycling. He has seen me take empty water bottles in the past and knows my routine."

"What did he say about being caught in a lie?"

"He used the old *brain fart* excuse." Judee paused and, in

a soft voice, said, "I am sorry I doubted you. I know you were following the evidence. I just did not want to believe a new friend could be so diabolical."

"Forget it. The important thing is for you to be careful. Dutronc may suspect we are on to him. Or, at least I am. If I am right, he is a nasty character."

"Thanks. We will be in a public place the whole time. I will not take Dutronc back to the lab. The lunch is his apology, then I will wash my hands of him."

"Still," said Hal.

"I get it," Judee said, "I'll be careful."

* * *

Sill was at a high table when Dutronc came in. He was all smiles as he walked over and climbed onto the chair. He reached over and put his hand in hers. Sill's immediate response was to pull her hand away, but she forced herself to accept the gesture. She offered a smile, suggesting she welcomed it.

"Thank you for agreeing to meet me today," Dutronc said. "It was wrong to deceive you. I should have told you I had been in Texas before San Antonio."

"Yes, you should have."

"But we were having such a wonderful time. I did not want to disrupt the experience. So I assumed that would be our only encounter."

"So, you were making a move on me?" Sill asked, attempting a smirk.

Still holding her hand, Dutronc looked Sill in the eye. "I'm French. What can I say? It is what we do. It is in our DNA."

Abruptly changing the subject, Sill said, "Let's get our meals. We can talk while we eat."

Dutronc got a Philly steak sub, and Judee got the Mediterranean bowl. The lunch was an obligatory response to recent events and not an enjoyable experience. To calm herself down, Sill excused herself and went to the restroom. She splashed water on her face and gave herself a pep talk in the mirror. She returned to find Dutronc had finished his sub and was smiling. He got up when she returned.

"Are you alright?" Dutronc asked with genuine concern.

"Just a lot going on right now," she said and took a sip of water.

"I'm sorry. I have an afternoon meeting in Austin, and I am the primary presenter. Therefore, I must leave now if I want to be on time."

"That's fine. Go. I don't want you to be late," Sill said. "More training?"

"Yes, Interpol is rolling out an updated, organized crime program, and I promised to share it with the Travis County Law Enforcement Council." Dutronc put the lid on the empty water bottle and got up.

"Let me have the bottle," Judee said as she took the it from him. "You know I recycle these things." Dutronc set the bottle on the table and left.

"I will call you before I head back to France. Then maybe you and your deputy friend can join me for dinner."

"We'll see. You understand Hal is a busy guy," she lied. She would be happy never to see his face again.

As he left, Dutronc reached to put his hand on Sill's. She did not pull it away, but picked up her fork to finish her salad bowl before returning to work.

"OK," he said. "Until the next time." Dutronc put his trash in the bin and set the plastic bowl on the shelf. In less than a minute, he was gone.

Judee put the empty bottle in an evidence bag she had brought with her. She put the bag in her purse, got out her phone, and called Blaine.

"He's gone, and I have the water bottle," she said.

"Good. How was it?" Blaine said with sympathy. He knew it was a hard lunch, especially after discovering Dutronc had lied.

"It was better than expected." Judee played with her salad. She had difficulty listening as Hal continued talking. When Hal hung up, she put a grape tomato in her mouth and bit down. Without warning, her face contorted. Her expression registered shock and terror, and she coughed twice. Then Sill fell off her chair.

CHAPTER 30

Dutronc sat in his nondescript gray Honda. He wanted to observe the unfolding of the events he started. He was confident the powder caused almost immediate illness. And as an expert with the poison, he was aware it was not a lethal dose. In his line of work, it was imperative to know how much arsenic is needed to disable a victim. And how much would be lethal. He liked this Texas medical examiner. He also understood with her tenacious deputy that caution was imperative.

Dutronc smiled upon seeing the sheriff's Suburban arrive on the scene before anyone else. Blaine ran into the restaurant just as a fire department engine and an ambulance arrived. Dutronc found it curious that the fire department always responded to these incidents. There was no fire, but there was that big red engine. He remained until the ambulance departed. Once the pedestrian traffic resumed, he pulled out and headed in the opposite direction.

The Austin training was a ruse, and he was fearful the boyfriend would show up. This deputy of hers had way too many questions for comfort. The Frenchman had greased enough palms to know they were closing in on him. He needed the safety of his home base where he could disappear. While his DNA was not in any database, his fingerprints were. He was confident they would not find his fingerprints at the Mexia fire. But, until today, no law enforcement agency had his DNA. He understood why Sill had chosen that restaurant because of the plastic bottle. Dutronc recognized the recycling move was also a ruse. Within days, the deputy would have his DNA. But was his DNA found at the fire? After the fire, he felt sure they could not trace it back to him. But with Judee wanting his water bottle, he sensed he had made a fatal error.

While Sill was in the lady's room, Dutronc had considered leaving. It was not the gentlemanly thing to do. But he had no illusions of ever seeing this lovely lady again. Dutronc did not expect her to take the plastic bottle, but found no way to keep it from her. The explanation seemed reasonable. Sill was big on recycling and it intrigued Dutronc when Sill would put trash in her bag. However, Dutronc also considered the consequences and became concerned. He hoped the bottle would not leave the restaurant in her purse.

Dutronc headed north to DFW International but did not return the car to the rental agency. Instead, he parked it in the garage nearest the AeroMéxico terminal. He then rode the shuttle bus to the Delta terminal for a flight to Quebec City. Jacques Dutronc was no longer on the road. Helmut Lotti, a baker from Quebec, was arriving home. But Helmut was soon on his way to limbo-land. Jonathan Vandenbroeck, an industrial salesman from Finland, was heading to Brazil for a vacation. It would take more than a month before Jonathan would relax on the famous Ipanema Beach. Along the way, Jacques Dutronc, Helmut Lotti, and Jonathan Vandenbroeck would travel and rent cars and hotels in multiple cities. Helmut might fly into Mexico City, but Jacques rents the car, and Jonathan reserves the hotel room.

Three months after arriving in Rio de Janeiro, Jonathan Vandenbroeck received an envelope. This caused concern. A bachelor with no family, no one from his past had heard from him since leaving Mexia. But there it was. 'Jonathan Vandenbroeck' had been written on the envelope.

"Where did this come from?" he asked his housekeeper.

"Some lady folded it in the gate. It had your name on it,"

she said.

"What did the lady look like?" he asked.

"Tall, thin, dark hair. Only saw her when she walked away."

Jonathan got a cold bottle of water and sat at the kitchen island. He opened the envelope and found two pieces of paper. The first was an international wanted poster for Jacques Dutronc, with the Helmut Lotti alias. "Good," he said to himself. "They don't know about Jonathan." He did not relax, though, because someone had found him. Dutronc set the poster aside and opened the other paper. It was the front page of a Paris newspaper. The lead story was the arrest of Lucio Dalla and Ross Bagdesarian.

Paris police have arrested two men with known ties to the Bagdesarian mafia family. They believe the two committed several murders dating back decades. A search of their Messina home revealed a small handgun. Tests confirmed it was the gun used in each of the murders in France, Italy, Spain, Portugal, and one in the United States.

A note written in French with a permanent marker said they were on house arrest
in Messina.

More than anything else, the envelope unnerved him. *How did they find him? Also, how did they know who he was?* And *who was this mysterious lady?* These two things provided a problem needing handling. He determined sooner rather than later.

Dutronc opened his satellite phone and punched in the numbers. But, of course, this number would be called only in a dire emergency.

"It's me," Dutronc said when the voice on the other end answered. "Ready?"

"Yes, sir."

"Best time?"

The voice was void of emotion. "Veranda, late afternoon."

"Three days," Dutronc said and ended the call.

* * *

Bagdesarian was not worried about his legal entanglement with the murders. He had solid alibis and knew neither he nor Dalla were in danger. To solidify this belief, the two agreed to provide incriminating evidence against corrupt Interpol officers, especially the rogue inspector Jacques Dutronc.

Dalla brought out two glasses of Dievole and a tray of meats, cheeses, and crackers. He gave one glass of wine to his friend and took a seat to enjoy the evening sky. The veranda looked out at acres of vines.

Dalla felt his phone vibrate and opened it. He read a message and then showed the phone to Bagdesarian. *Contract out for Bagdesarian. Careful.*

"Sure glad I am secure in this little villa of ours," said Bagdesarian. "I never thought house arrest would be so restful."

"Yes. We are under the watchful eye of the Guardia de Finanza. They want to make sure we are available for trial."

"My friend, what trial?" They clinked glasses and took a sip of wine. Dalla watched his friend put a piece of salami and gouda on a cracker. A small red dot appeared on Bagdesarian's forehead when he put the food in his mouth. Dalla recognized it as a sniper's laser, but said nothing. Then, the dot got larger for a few seconds as Bagdesarian's head snapped backward. The move would have broken the man's neck if he were still alive. Instead, the last dot ensured the man felt no pain.

Dalla stood and faced the area where he knew the sniper was supposed to be. He gave a thumbs up and raised his glass to the field. He was unaware there was the same red dot on his forehead. Before he could swallow the sip of wine in his mouth, the hole in his head got larger. And just as with his boss, his head snapped back, and he fell to the deck.

"No loose ends," said the sniper with a smile.

There was no sound, and their guards were unaware of what had happened. The sniper was aware of the guards' routine. He knew it would be thirty minutes before they would find the bodies. He would be long gone by then.

The sniper disassembled his rifle and put it back in the case. Showing no signs of urgency, he ensured there were no cigarette butts on the ground. He destroyed the visible footprints. The sniper then headed down to where his driver was waiting in the new Citroen C5 X.

The trunk and the rear door were open when he reached the road. He put the gun case in the trunk, got in, and closed the door.

"Where to, Mr. Dutronc?" asked the driver.

"Palermo," said Dutronc.

Dutronc noticed the driver did not move the car. "What are you waiting for?" he asked.

"Can't go," said the driver.

"And why not?" demanded Dutronc.

"We have company." A policeman was standing at the front of the car. *Where did he come from?* Dutronc said to himself. At that moment, he was aware of sirens. Both in front and at the back of the car. He could see the flashing blue lights heading toward him. Dutronc turned to see three cars pull up behind. The officer at the front of the car walked to where he sat. Both rear doors opened, and six Carabinieri had guns pointed at him.

A tall man stood behind the three on the car's passenger side. "Jacques Dutronc, Helmut Lotti, and Jonathan Vandenbroeck. You are under arrest for the murders of Bruno Ughi and Sergio Galli. Out of the car, please."

Dutronc did not get out of the car. Instead, addressing the tall man in charge, he asked, "Miss Sill? Is she alright?"

"Yes, with no thanks to you."

"Good, I liked her. She is a good person."

"You sure have a funny way of showing it."

Then two officers reached in and yanked Dutronc out of

the car.

* * *

Bill Fries had given a heads-up to Blaine about the morning's call. Blaine had his team in the room when the FBI agent rang.

"Good morning, Bill," said Hal when answering the phone. It was a conference call, so that everyone could join in.

"Hey, Hal, everybody there?"

They all announced their presence.

"It's over. We have Dutronc in a federal jail in Florence."

"Any problems?"

"We were too late, and his kill number escalated by two. Although Bagdesarian and Dalla received protection from the Italian police, both are dead," said Fries.

"Agent Fries, Sheriff Hazelwood here. What happens now?"

"The Italian judicial system moves more quickly than ours. So Dutronc, or whatever he calls himself, will stand trial next month."

"For two murders?" This came from Chief Musselwhite.

"Four. Bagdesarian, Dalla, Ughi and Galli," responded Fries.

"What will he get?" asked Sill.

"My guess is it will be in the neighborhood of two hundred years. Murderers often get fifty years. There are four murders, and in these cases, the convicted serve them consecutively."

"Any chance of parole?" asked Blaine.

"No such thing in Italy. They must serve the full amount," assured Fries.

"Any chance of sentence reduction?"

Fries laughed and said, "What reduction? He goes to France and faces murder charges there if he gets out early. And don't forget Spain, Portugal, and the United States indicted him for murder."

"So," Hazelwood said, "It is over."

"Yes, but it is only through the tenacity of your deputy,

sheriff. If Hal's stomach had not reacted…" There was soft laughter. "And if your team had not done such a thorough job, we would not be having this conversation." Everyone cheered and applauded. When the noise subsided, Fries said, "We can't forget the special contribution your fabulous medical examiner made. I'm just glad Dutronc liked her enough not to kill her."

"You're not the only one," Hal said, looking at his medical examiner.

* * *

Friday night, Blaine's yellow Camaro pulled up to Sill's house. Before he could knock, the door opened.

"Did I miss something? I thought we were supposed to go dancing," Blaine asked.

"That is still an option."

"So, there is another option?" wondered Hal.

"Yes," Sill said. She kissed him and put her arms around his neck.

"Wow!"

"Well," she said, smiling up at him. "You said you wanted to continue the conversation we started the last time we went out."

"Sound good to me," he said. He kicked the door shut with his foot, put his arms around her, and drew her into him. "Let's talk!"

EPILOGUE

Deputy Hal Blaine had been the center of a media maelstrom for three months. Everyone wanted to know about this rookie deputy sheriff from a small Texas town. The one who brought down an international serial killer. The major media outlets in the States had him on their shows. *Today, Good Morning America, CBS Mornings,* and *Fox & Friends* all had him as a guest. Even a major European media outlet fussed over him.

Things settled down, allowing Mexia and Limestone County to return to normal. The London-based FBI agent, Bill Fries, was in the States for a family get-together in California. He stopped by Mexia to see his old friend and meet the team that made everything possible. They were at the Cattlemen in Fort Worth for a celebratory meal.

"Hal, I can't figure out how you did it," said Fries, showing his pride for his friend. "He had been murdering people for three decades. And a rookie deputy sheriff closed a half-dozen cold cases in a few months. Something police in four countries couldn't do in forty years. How?"

"The number one reason serial killers get caught is?" asked Hal.

Fries answered, "Ego. They think they are beyond the reach of the law."

"Bingo! Dutronc could steer the police investigating these homicides in a direction that kept his identity a secret."

"But they knew him," said Sill.

"Yes. The various departments knew Dutronc, the Interpol investigator. However, they were unaware of Dutronc, the murderer."

Sheriff Hazelwood added, "He had done such a good job he was unafraid to point a rookie deputy in his direction."

"Right on, sheriff," Fries said. "He felt he had buried his association with these murders and believed Hal would never catch on."

"What about the first murder?" AK asked. "They did not link him to that murder."

"Not until Hal got me thinking."

"You got the lightbulb lit, did you?" asked Blaine and lifted his beer to the FBI agent.

"Hal kept chipping away until he found a connection to your murder."

"It wasn't Hal. It was me," said Sill. "And I told a lie. Y'all forgive me?"

Hal was sitting next to his medical examiner. He lifted her hand and kissed the back of it. "You are forgiven. Trust me on that."

Laughing at Hal's gesture and Sill's comment, Fries continued. "Dutronc did not know it was a lie. He believed Dr. Sill learned the truth and improvised."

"And I almost died," said Sill, slapping Hal's chest as she said this.

"Ah, my love, you were always safe."

"What did you say?"

"You were always safe." Hal did not look at her, knowing what she heard.

"You called me your love. I have witnesses. I am your love. Try to back out of it now, buddy!" Sill leaned into him.

"You cooked your goose now," said Hazelwood.

"Big-time," said Chief Musselwhite.

"I plead the fifth!" said Hal.

"Too late," said AK. "Too many witnesses."

"Whatever," said Fries, trying to refocus the conversation. "I began backtracking Dutronc's career. He was a police officer in Paris assigned to the other side of town."

"Why? Why did he kill Chevalier?"

"Revenge. We discovered the old man was a mercenary, available to the highest bidder. Parkinson's set in, and he had trouble holding the gun steady. A minor stroke meant he dragged his left foot. He was an easy mark for a young, eager-to-please Dutronc."

"Motive?" asked Hazelwood.

"It seems Bagdesarian's father hired Chevalier to kill the boy's mother, kidnap the lad, and deliver him to his father."

"So, Bagdesarian hired Dutronc?" asked Musselwhite between bites.

"Yes. He was looking to establish his identity as an assassin. He and Bagdesarian knew each other after Bagdesarian escaped his father's controlling hand. Both lived on the streets of Paris."

"If both were on the street, where did the money come from?" asked Blaine.

"Bagdesarin's dad. His dad was wealthy, and old Ross did not leave home empty-handed. He took a small handgun from the house along with the money and gave Dutronc the weapon and cash."

"Then what?" asked AK.

"Bagdesarian paid for a flat for the two of them, and they cleaned up their act and appearances. Dutronc used his brains to get into the Paris police force. The Chevalier murder was a test run. Could he do it and get away with it?"

"And he did," said Musselwhite.

"Bagdesarian was a natural con man and weaseled his way into organized crime."

"And the rest is history," said Sill.

"What triggered Dutronc to kill A.C.? We could not establish a motive," said Hal.

"Mr. Ragsdale provided the answer. A.C. was in Austin

when he saw Bergman, Dalla and Bagdesarian together."

"And we determined Dutronc was in the area when the murder happened," said Blaine.

"Yes. Hoping for leniency, Dutronc has been quite the canary. He saw Mottola and recognized him. Whether Mottola saw Dutronc, we will never know. But Dutronc believed A.C. recognized him."

"Why did that matter?" asked a confused AK.

"Ragsdale told you. Some hacker leaked his and Mottola's identities and family identities," Fries said.

"And Dutronc was the hacker," concluded Hazelwood.

"Exactamundo."

"But Ragsdale said they were unsure who it was."

"Again, that was a fact Dutronc didn't have. Mr. Mottola was within earshot when Dutronc's guest called him by name. It is possible Mottola reacted to the name. Thus, to keep everything intact Mottola needed to be eliminated."

"OK, why poison me?" asked Sill. "And why only enough to make me sick? He had to understand you were on to him."

"He did. But he listened to his heart," said Fries. "According to the Italian Police, he was concerned for your health. When arrested, the first thing he did was to ask if you were OK. He admitted he did not want to kill you."

"Well, that was sweet of him," said Sill with sarcasm.

"He liked you. A lot!" said Fries. "And he realized you and your deputy here," pointing to Blaine, "were in a romantic relationship."

"We were not!" protested Hal.

"Oh, but we were. Remember the conversation we started?" Sill said and winked at Blaine.

"What conversation?" they all asked.

Holding his hands up to ward off an evil spirit, "There was no conversation." Then, turning to Sill, Hal said, "Was there?!"

"My lips are sealed," and Sill made a zipper motion across her closed lips.

"What about now?" asked Hazelwood. "Everyone knows your yellow bird, and there are multiple reports of it at Sill's house for extended periods."

"And I have noticed her blue Tesla in front of your house," said AK, pointing to Blaine.

"OK, OK, OK. We once in a while, we see each other outside of work."

"A lot," said the sheriff.

"Maybe," said Blaine, looking at the sheriff. "I have never used the L-word."

"Liar!" said Sill.

"When?"

"Tonight."

"Tonight?"

Sill had him on the ropes and was enjoying every minute. "You said to me, and I quote, *My Love!*"

"That doesn't count," said a stammering Hal. "Does it?"

Everyone said the same thing in unison for the second time that evening. "Yup!"

Everyone laughed and let Hal off the hook. They talked about Fries' assignment in London, his family, and many mundane things. Sheriff Hazelwood surprised everyone when he picked up the tab. Hal and Judee followed Bill back to his hotel and visited in the bar for another hour. Finally, they said their goodnights and goodbyes. Fries headed to his room. Blaine and Sill drove to her house in silence.

At Judee's house, Hal grabbed her and held her tight. "Shall we continue the conversation inside?"

"Not until you say the L-word." She held her right index finger to his lips. And in a quiet voice, added, "and mean it."

Hal wrapped his arms around her. Then cheek-to-cheek, he whispered, "I love you."

Steve Wilcox is a retired schoolteacher. In addition to his classroom duties, he coached junior high football, wrestling and track. He had directed more than 50 plays and spent a decade coaching high school mock trial. He and his wife have been married for more than 50 years and have two grown children and two granddaughters. This is his fourth book, second novel, and first murder mystery. He calls Hewitt, Texas home.

COMING SOON

THE PAINTING
A Ted James Novel

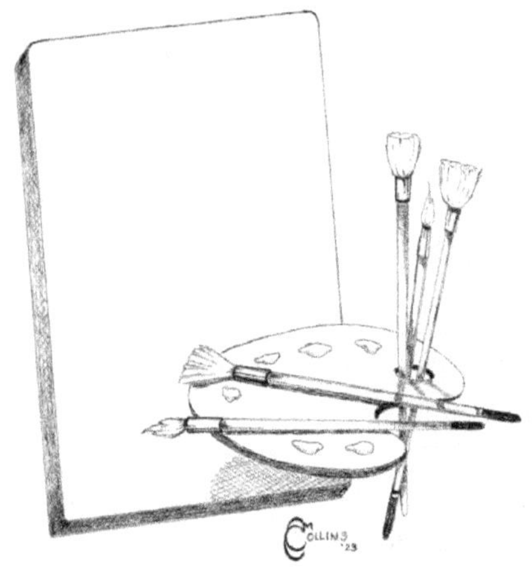

Allora Hughes lies in a coma following an auto accident. As friends and family pray for her recovery, she is granted the rare opportunity to have a conversation with God. When she awakes, she is a new woman with a new purpose. She must ask for forgiveness for the wrongs she has done, but she must forgive those who have hurt her. This included the drink driver who caused the accident killing her father. As she grows in her new-found faith, she feels and urge to recreate DaVinci's masterpiece of The Last Supper. Only, her version will have Jesus and the apostles in modern dress and have faces of those important in her life.

Allora turned her back on God following the death of her father. Now, she will use this painting to return home as a child of God.